Redemption Veil

Travis Summerville

Editor: Terrie Scott

ISBN: **978-0-9998347-0-1**

Printed in the United States of America

To Sean and Mike - thanks for pushing my imagination, through dark twisting catacombs, fantastical landscapes, beyond far horizons and always off the map.

Acknowledgements

I would like to thank Terrie Scott, my Editor, who helped me as a brand new author put a story out into the world.

I would like to thank Chris Scalf for the cover art. He is an incredible artist and a deeply creative soul.

To the late Robert Monroe, who showed me that
'I am more than my physical body.'

Chapter 1

Fire, Swords, and Darkness

Bargavon stumbled into the cool darkness. How he got here he did not know, his brain felt like it was on fire and his eyes were having a hard time adjusting to the dim light of the gloom about him. It was if he were in a cave or an ancient temple, so old that the stonework was eroding away. Up ahead was a warm light reflecting off of a wall of old pitted dark stone. He made his way around a corner to view what appeared to be a chamber. The floor was a glow of red and orange burning coals casting warm colored light across the darkened walls that rose up into the darkness. His eyes followed the floating orange embers from the coals upward into this darkness and there above. His eyes adjusted slowly to take in the vastness of a star filled sky. A sky that was strange and unfamiliar. So deep was its blackness he felt as if his hand left the wall he traced that he would be pulled up into the vastness above.

His reverie was cut short by the growl of a great cat behind him. Bargavon whirled around drawing forth his sword in one smooth motion. Behind him emerging from the dark gloom was a large black jaguar. Its size was great. The cat's yellow eyes seemed to glow. Its teeth bared stark white and a low growl vibrated from its throat. It stopped several feet away and waited. Bargavon didn't move. His reflexes and fighting skills were good, but he knew better than to make the first move. It was better to react to the jaguar's lunge and sidestep with a sword thrust. After a few moments, the jaguar raised its head and seemed to nod toward the coals, as if it expected Bargavon to cross.

Bargavon looked over his shoulder quickly at the coals. *Is this thing giving me a choice, a choice of death? Too wide, can't make the jump. I'll be burned alive trying to make it across that width.* Bargavon turned back and met the gaze of the black beast. In the cat's eyes, he seemed to have been given an answer.

"You must do this. It is the only way."

As if sensing his hesitation, the jaguar roared out and displayed his teeth showing his displeasure. He took a step forward and roared again, as if trying to intimidate Bargavon into hopelessly crossing the burning coals. Baragvon held his ground defiantly and finally, the jaguar started forward taking a swipe with razor-sharp claws. Bargavon dropped and weaved from the blow and as he tried to follow with a counterstrike with his sword, the cat beat him to the mark and caught him in his jaws. It crushed his throat and the sword fell from his grasp. Instead of snapping his neck, the cat dragged him near the coals.

Bargavon gasped for air that did not come, his hands grasped and pounded at the massive black cat but to no avail. *This is how I die, and I don't even know how I got here and for what? Why this?*

As he was losing consciousness, he felt a sharp rip within him, as if his entire being had been opened up and laid bare. He could feel part of him being pulled away. He assumed he was being disemboweled and mauled by the claws of the cat. Suddenly, he was aware that the cat released the death grip and sauntered away nearby. The cat sat upright and watched him with keen interest. Bargavon coughed and took in a great lungful of air. He was afraid to look down at the eviscerated ruin of his body, probably the last sight he would see before death took him. Instead, he was whole, not a wound upon him. The feeling of being ripped open quickly subsided to a dull ache deep within him.

There was a sound to his left as he slowly propped himself up on an elbow. Next to him was a figure of a man, jet black and in armor with clothing the same as he, but he appeared nothing more than a black solid silhouette. He was literally the spitting image of Bargavon. It too was slowly rising, as it rolled over to face him. Bargavon was chilled to the bone looking as a shadow of him became solid. Its eyes opened as two ovals, deep red in color and upon seeing Bargavon they showed a sudden recognition. His mouth opened revealing a row of sharp predatory fangs in place of teeth. An evil hiss and growl ushered from its maw. There was something about this demon doppelganger that repulsed Bargavon, something deep and intangible that was beyond just the demonic figure.

"Cross the fire, both of you together. It is the only way now" echoed a voice that seemed to call out from beyond the other side of the coals. Bargavon looked up to see through the wavering orange glow of the heat the vague image of a man in a loincloth holding a staff. Next to him, sat the great black jaguar. It's eyes aglow, waiting.

How did that cat get through the fire? The distance was too far even for it, and who is that man?

Bargavon had no further time to contemplate. He was aware that the dark figure stood now and looked menacing in the firelight. It issued strange gravelly rasps and hisses, as if learning how to create speech. Bargavon quickly rolled, grabbed up his sword from the ground and leaped to attack the dark menace.

The Dark Warrior responded and drew forth his own blade of impenetrable blackness and brought it lashing down upon Bargavon. He parried it away. Bargavon was a trained warrior and killer. He crouched and swept his leg out and tangled his dark doppelganger's legs causing him to stumble and sent him reeling backward several feet before recovering. It was enough time for Baragvon to quickly assess his adversary. In all respects, he seemed a viscous solid black shadow of himself right down to the same type of sword he held, except that he carried it in the left hand.

The dark figure charged him. It seethed and raged. The hate and viciousness flowed out from him. The sword work was no less than Bargavon's best however, and he was hard pressed to parry and dodge the blows while finding his own openings to try and land strikes. Both warriors clashed blades in a fast and desperate life or death battle. Both warriors had drawn blood for it poured onto the ground between them. Fatigue and desperation began to weigh upon them. Swordsmanship wore away to wild swings and sloppy parries, staggering attacks and retreats until they could no longer hold firm their weapons. Finally, it came to close in grappling and both fell to the ground choking each other out in a death embrace. Bargavon was upon his back, the dark figure had a vice-like grasp upon his throat, but he himself was hard pressed as Bargavon's thumbs gouged slowly deeper into the Dark Warrior's own.

With great effort the dark figure heaved up Baragvon and shoved him into the edge of the burning coals. Bargavon cried out as the searing heat began to blister the side of his neck and shoulder. With a last surge of strength, Bargavon thrust up beneath his dark straddling enemy and rolled him over full onto the burning coalfield.

Screams of rage and pain burst forth from the dark figure as he gained his footing and plunged back out of the fire, flames trailing from him as he staggered back. Bargavon hauled himself up with great effort and stumbled over to again retrieve his sword, but the dark warrior had enough and staggered away into the dark corridor from which Bargavon had initially entered the chamber. Catching his breath, he looked back across the burning coals to see the man in the loincloth meet his gaze then slowly walk away into the darkness. The great black jaguar continued to sit there, a flicker of amusement seemed to dance across its glowing yellow eyes.

Seeing no further way out but the way he came, Bargavon stumbled back down the passage of darkness that originally brought him here. Expecting to find his dark foe ready to fight him again or its burned dead body, Bargavon found neither and soon found himself into a dark gloom. The pain, loss of blood and fatigue were causing his head to spin and soon his legs gave way. He felt his body collapse against what felt like cool stone. His vision completely blackened and the last thing he perceived was the sound of his own rasping breath before unconsciousness took him. His mind posed one last contemplative thought, *And, so I die, for what?*

Chapter 2

The Temple and the Shaman

Bargavon awoke sprawled upon his back atop a crumbled slab of stone. Fresh blood was pooled underneath him and dripped down onto the stony ground that was covered profusely by both moss and vine. His vision was blurry, and he hurt all over. He sat up from the slab fighting a wave of nausea and looked around. He appeared to be atop a hill, the jungle canopy easily half a hundred feet below. Nearby a cave mouth the height of a man yawned open at the peak of the hill. The morning sun was breaking over steamy clouds revealed the cave was no deeper than several feet and that it was instead a man-made chamber of closely fitted stone. Something was atop this stone structure. Through the blur he could see it was a great cat. A spotted jaguar and it was keenly watching him. It got up from a crouch without taking its eyes off of him. It sat for a moment then turned and dropped out of sight behind the structure.

Bargavon's sight was starting to come into focus but what was garnering most of his attention now was a raging burning pain across his neck and shoulder. It felt burned and blistered. Several bleeding cuts were also present upon him. The pain worsened with his effort of sitting upright upon the slab. His wounds were not mortal, nor were they too deep but deep enough and the move from lying to sitting caused what little clotting had been done to reopen and bleed a fresh coat of blood down his trunk. What was left of his tattered shirt he decided to make into a makeshift bandage to cover his wounds.

He was dizzy and had trouble piecing together last night's events. He remembered the fight against the dark warrior which despite being fresh to memory retained an unreal dreamlike quality, despite the painful evidence to the contrary. He vaguely remembered a shipwreck, some heavy drinking, sleeping with a dark haired beauty, and some more fighting. Not that any of that was unusual, except maybe the shipwreck part and the nightmare-like fight with the dark warrior. Nothing was coming together in a linear timeline and his whereabouts completely escaped him. As his vision started to focus better, his mind started to coalesce. First, the air was hot and humid, steamy actually. Second, his vision cleared to reveal that he stood not upon a hill but upon an ancient pyramid, partially draped under the effects of the continuous march of time and nature. Jungle trees and vines had asserted themselves in cracks and crevasses, moss grew in the shadowy areas. Animals and birds found places to roost or burrow transforming what was once a magnificent man-made pyramid into a frame for the proliferation of life.

The small shrine which moments ago served as a throne for a jaguar appeared to have chamber within. Bargavon fought through nausea, a pounding headache and his wounds to stand up and stumble over to the wide mouth of the chamber. Inspection revealed only some bones, broken baked clay pottery, and a simple stone platform. Etchings in the walls may have been runes or pictures but erosion and decay wore the carvings down to imperceptible scratches with the exception of what appeared to be the outline of a doorway. There was fresh blood on this surface which

Bargavon noted matched the height of his wounds. *Perhaps a secret door I had passed through, must have leaned against the doorway as I came through.* He pushed a little and spent a few minutes examining the etched doorway, thumping a fist or kicking against it. *Seems like solid stone.*

Making no further progress he stepped out of the small structure and found that he could make his way around it. He half expected to encounter his last moments on earth to end in the jaws of a jaguar but found something rather curious. The temple literally dropped away into a sheer drop-off. The stone wall of the small structure on top was flush with the drop-off. The etched doorway was simply that….an engraving. There could be no physical passage beyond. *Perhaps I thought it was a door and rubbed up against it……and where was the jaguar? They are known to leap and climb trees, but the distance down seems too far unless it can scale the sheer rock wall……perhaps…..possible.*

A pounding headache, nausea and blood loss are not conducive for deep thinking and, so he took stock in more immediate matters. Bargavon realized besides wearing just tatters of clothes, his mail shirt was missing, but he found his sword and scabbard nearby. Drawing it out, it was covered in fresh blood. *Perhaps it is my own and these wounds of mine were self-inflicted. Possibly, but why?* He was able to replay the desperate fight with the dark warrior in his mind simply by grasping the sword hilt as if the tactile sensation jogged fully his memory of what seemed like a nightmare.

Who was the dark warrior that seemed to literally embody a sinister viscous shadow version of himself, the field of flaming burning coals, the great black jaguar and the man with the staff. Again, his thoughts tried to piece together where the fight took place and how did he end up there or even here for that matter? He had questions, no answers, increasing pain from moving about and now a burning thirst.

The morning sun was turning from orange to a blazing yellow as its light poured across the jungle canopy turning the dark foliage to brilliant shades of greens. The songbirds began to fill the morning quietude along with the more raucous squawks of larger birds and screeches of monkeys unseen in the trees.

Bargavon carefully picked his way down a terrifyingly steep set of ancient steps running down the pyramid's face. The steps seemed to be just a bit too steep and the footing too shallow. *Did the builders of this ancient monument have extra-long legs with tiny feet?* To make matters worse, the steamy jungle air made the stone steps slick with humidity feeding the patches of moisture hungry moss or lichen. If he pitched forward, he was a dead man. His fears were justified as he passed several skeletons and human bones wedged in broken slabs of upturned rock or grown through by leafy vines or an entwining tree root seeking pockets of captured water in the eroded temple stonework.

A small python pulled itself through the skeletal rib cage of a one of the previous unfortunates and paused only a moment to consider the nearby human clambering down the pyramid face was still too big to be within her part of the food chain. Bargavon did reach the bottom and sat for a moment nauseous from effort, loss of blood and dehydration. At the base he was mildly delighted to see footprints in the wet earth. Namely his footprints, Imperial Army issued sandal prints. He could see the track was zig-zagged as if he had been drunk and stumbling. What was a little unnerving was a set of tracks paralleling his. These were most likely a big cat. Perhaps that jaguar that mysteriously vanished. Not sure if it was following close or if it came long after him. *Maybe he led me here* mused Bargavon at the silly thought.

"You were led here Medregorian." Came a dry highly accented voice from behind him. Bargavon jumped and spun about startled. In doing so the world spun too fast and he almost passed out. His spinning vision caught sight of a tall deeply brown elderly man who was sitting just a few steps up the temple from where he had been. How Bargavon had missed him on his way down could only be guessed at. The elderly man was quite nimble as he bounded down from his step to reach out and catch Bargavon, preventing him from planting face first on the jungles carpet of green moss and tree roots.

Pain and nausea were so strong that Bargavon allowed the man to assist him back down to rest his head against the temple step. The old man pulled out a gourd "Drink this," he ordered. Bargavon simply complied, he was just too weak to argue. It was water and he drank most of it down.

When he finished he was able to give his full attention to the man. He was a little taller than Bargavon, thin and wiry with deep brown skin, etched by time and sun. His eyes were a strange mix of blue and brown that together lent them a peculiar hue. Old tattoos lined his face, his arms and his legs all the way down to his feet. He wore no sandals. He wore only a long loincloth, and carried an animal hide rucksack and a staff that curved at the top and from which all sorts of Shamanic paraphernalia hung; small bones, a bird's claw, teeth, a few small pouches, a small bundle of herbs, some colored feathers and a few polished stones with holes drilled in them to lace to the staff by fibrous thongs. *He looks somewhat like that man in my nightmare.*

"Don't move warrior. Your wounds are bad, but they will not kill you. You need them closed and that burn tended to." As he said this he pulled from his bag a bone needle and some long strands of plant fiber. Bargavon understood. He had received many wounds on the battlefield and was used to being stitched up. The old man got to work and the sharp needle work made Bargavon wince but he questioned the man through his tight grimace.

"You are not Medregorian, but you can speak it. Who are you? I saw you in a dream last night standing on the other side of a bed of hot coals"

"My name is Mokantai. I originally hailed from the nomads of the High Subharian Desert. I learned to speak your Imperial tongue as a youth in the caravans that crossed it." The elderly man continued to sew up the wounds and when finished opened up a small flask and poured a foul smelling liquid across the incisions. It burned and Bargavon grimaced further.

"For the healing. It will keep out rot," he explained placing a bandage made of some colored clay-like paste and then a few fibrous looking bandages. Upon another large leaf he poured out a sap and then placed this over the burn. It felt cool and soothing.

"You are a long way from the desert," said Bargavon drinking a bit more slowly from the water gourd.

"I came here to study the medicine practices of the jungle tribes many years ago, was taken in as an apprentice under a great Shaman and I have been here ever since. After the passing of my master, I was made Shaman by the tribes here. Even though I'm a Subharian, the tribal elders have made me an official Untari. I wander among all of the Untari tribal territories seeing to their needs." Mokanti surveyed his handiwork and seemed satisfied.

"How did I get here? I remember a storm that wrecked me off the coast and I made it into the jungle for protection from the storm. I knew the coastal jungle was thick with cannibal tribes so I dared not enter too far but I do remember being chased by a band of tribesmen that chased me deeper in than I should have gone…….." Bargavon's headache was easing a bit allowing more coherent thought. "I remember now. There was a tribal village and I was met by some tribesmen with spears. As I was trying to show them I was no threat, my pursuers must have tracked me there, because they showed up right after and all hell broke loose. Apparently, they were enemies of the village and both of those groups started fighting. I remember the village men were not numerous and were outnumbered almost three to one. I decided to throw my lot in with the villagers and helped drive those bastards hunting me off. I killed many of them myself. Perhaps they were not use to a steel sword and chainmail. I think the villagers were impressed because they actually allowed me to enter the village after the fight. It kind of goes quite vague after that."

"Then let me fill you in Medregorian." The Shaman's face soured. "From what I am told, you entered my hut and accidentally drank a very special preparation I had made for my apprentice. Perhaps you mistook it for water or wine. That is what your people are so fond of drinking." The Shaman's eyes narrowed further and his voice took on a more scolding tone "That preparation took me a whole season to concoct. It was made with some of the strongest psychedelic and magical substances in the jungle. A Shaman's apprentice is given this draught one time in his entire lifetime to pass the last test to become a Shaman. The physical, mental, and spiritual preparation takes them a year to complete and they do this in solitude deep in the jungle mountains in ancient caves and shrines dedicated to this pursuit and used for millennia of Shamans since the dawn of time."

"I thought that wine tasted bad. You should add something to it to sweeten it up. It's pretty bitter. Well, that explains the headache and nausea and I must of blackout out." Mused Bargavon scratching the stubble on his chin.

The Shaman's eyes popped out in a glare at the insult and general ambivalence of the consequences of the Medregorian warrior drinking the sacred drink. The Shaman's anger was but a flash, but the scolding continued "Medregorian, do you realize that after you drank the contents of that gourd, you proceeded to take the virginity of the Chief's daughter, her two female attendants and injuring four more men of the village that tried to stop you. Then you burned down the Chief's hut and claimed yourself King of the Jungle!"

Bargavon took all this in for a moment. He did remember the tribal women part somewhat now and sure wished he remembered more of that, but the rest completely escaped him. *Getting in a tribal melee, drinking the mother of all mind-blowing beverages, bedding three women, one of whom is the chief's daughter, burning down the chief's hut and general mayhem in a village all by myself. Certainly, a productive night even for me.*

"What happened after that?"

"I convinced the villagers not to kill you. You would be dead, but the chief and all his warriors are away meeting with several of the other tribes about what to do about recent cannibal raids on the villages. Seeing that you drank the elixir I had prepared for my apprentice I led you to where I would have led him. The ancient temple before us here. The Jaguar God was waiting, and you were going to have a mystical vision quest like it or not. Unprepared as you were, death was most likely the outcome and I figured you probably deserved it but somehow you managed to survive the ordeal. Probably better that you died."

Bargavon looked at him thoughtfully, "You were there. You saw what happened on the temple; the flaming coals, the fight with the dark warrior."

"Initiates into Shaman-hood are required to walk through the fire coals and thus purify themselves and burn off the layers of negativity that cloud their heart and mind. You did not and you arrived there unprepared carrying within you a lifetime of deeply hidden pain and darkness. You however, are broken and fragmented. All this happened beyond the veil of this world, not on top of the temple. That holy place is just the portal into the realm beyond," the Shaman explained looking up toward the pyramid summit.

Bargavon's head swam taking in the gravity of the Shaman's statements, part of him did not believe any of it, but the wounds upon his body said otherwise. "Who was that dark warrior that left me these wounds to remember him by?"

"He is a broken fragment of you. He carries something, a great pain or secret from your past that was buried. Had you crossed the coals it may have been purified and integrated within you. Ignorant and stubborn you resisted, now I am not sure what to do with you, but a solution may present itself as they have a tendency to do. I, however, am surprised to see the wounds upon you. I have never seen wounds physically carry back over from beyond the Veil. Perhaps they resulted because you fought yourself. Interesting," mused Mokantai.

"You said you led me here, but I see only my footprints and that of a large cat that probably tracked my scent up the temple," pointed Bargavon to the set of tracks just beyond them leading from a jungle trail.

The Shaman turned toward the jungle trail as he placed his medicines back in his bag. "Hmmm, yes. So I did." He ignored further explanation. "Come we will talk on the way to the village. I have a hut there that has my remedies. Also, you have stepped into the vastness beyond the Veil. You will need me to help guide you and help you understand your experience. You are spiritually fragmented, and you will need to become whole again. Not an easy task."

He stood up feeling a little better, the headache was diminished somewhat, the wounds were at least dressed and he wasn't bleeding anymore, but the nausea still persisted. Bargavon followed Mokantai, lost in his thoughts for some time. *I suppose he doesn't want me dead, so I guess we'll see where he takes me. Hopefully, I can get back to the coast. Maybe the fleet has sent some ships to comb for survivors.* His thought was interrupted by the feeling and intensity of the images of the fight with the dark figure, the flames and the glowing eyes of the great black jaguar. A cold chill went up his spine and broke the humid perspiration that drenched his body.

They had gone a short ways down the trail when Mokantai's dry voice broke in over the background noise of chirping birds, and the occasional screech of a monkey. "Your things warrior."

His chain-mailed shirt laid crumpled in a heap upon the ground, as well as his dagger. His dagger was special to him. Not an Imperial army issued dagger which was light, slim and double-edged. No, this was a heavy blade. A dagger not only made for killing, but also for utility. It was a dagger carried by the barbarians along the Northern Marches. A heavy, wide-bodied blade that was double-edged, but was saw-toothed on the lower half of one side. Not only was this great for gouging out bigger holes in an adversary, but also useful for utility work such as sawing into meat or bone, cutting thick rope, hide or even small branches. Bargavon had taken this blade off a dead barbarian king he had slain in battle up in the Tondra Pass. This dagger had special markings, engraved on one side of the blade a raven, on the other a wolf. Common symbols for the Northmen who thought the animals imbued certain 'spirit' qualities. This dagger had no precious stone or gold in the pommel, and other than the engravings, it was just reliable. He inspected his mailed shirt. No damage or missing links except for some splinters of wood wedged in a few places, obvious remnants from fighting the cannibals. Why it was here instead of on him puzzled him. He clearly had it on during the fight with the dark warrior.

Mokantai perceived Bargavon's puzzlement, "You tore it off and dumped it here while under the influence of the potion. You may remember wearing it beyond the Veil, however. Our personal reflections of whom and what we are carry with us beyond. You would expect to be armed and armored and so you were."

He decided to don the mail shirt. Its 14 pounds would be better displaced over his frame than carrying it. It wouldn't be particularly comfortable, however, as he was missing his padded shirt.

The Shaman patiently waited for Bargavon to don the mail and strap the dagger to his belt. "Mail might be handy against the spear thrust of an angry chief." Smiled Bargavon weakly. He fought a wave of nausea for a moment, and thought, *who am I kidding. I am in no shape to fight.*

"It is my intention to get to my hut, gather what I need and get you out of the village before the chief and his warriors get back. Even I do not think I could stem Chief Ukko's wrath. But one challenge at a time warrior. I still have to get you to the village and we will most likely be met by Anaghandra."

"Anaghandra, sounds important. Anything I should know?" inquired Bargavon sensing the Shaman was holding back a bit. Mokantai kept walking at a steady pace not taking his eyes off the trail ahead.

"Well, Medregorian. You have managed through all that mayhem from the previous night, passed through the Veil, tore yourself in two and tried to murder yourself in front of the Jaguar God. Mystical initiation rituals do not normally proceed like this. We will see what Anaghandra has to say about you and what council he can give us."

"This Anaghandra is another Shaman?"

"No, but he has been around a very long time. He has seen many things over many ages."

Bargavon did not believe in gods. His own people had ninety-nine of them in their pantheon. He never saw any of them or any gods of his enemies although he had seen strange creatures and fantastic beasts in far off lands but nothing 'god-like,' however.

The path opened up to a clearing where a waterfall cascaded down into a large pool. Above the cliff thirty feet up was a massive thick limbed tree. Its heavy branches were like woody bridges spanning hundreds of feet in all directions. Great clumps of verdant green moss and vines hung from the heavy limbs and its great canopy was dark and foreboding. Bargavon noted no birds nor monkeys were in the trees. Before the pool were piles of rocks stacked up in primitive altars. Upon them, faded dark stains, probably blood, thought Bargavon. One of the rock structures was a large carven boulder of black basalt. It was eroded somewhat from ages, but one could still make out what appeared to be a snake faced man in ceremonial attire. What he thought was a great cowl behind his head he realized was a cobra hood. Mokantai stopped here at the carven basalt stone and waited. Bargavon said nothing but stood next to him. He felt the expectation of something ancient stirring as palpable as the steamy humidity that clung to him.

Bargavon was aware of a presence within the dark foliage, something big, dangerous and old. There was movement within the gloom and then his eyes detected a massive sinuous form move out from the dark onto one of the thick moss-covered branches. The body was dull black, with smooth scales that were mesmerizing with its sinuous movement. Its head appeared and was bigger than any snake Bargavon had ever seen. Its massive hood identified it as a king cobra, but of colossal proportions. He had seen king cobras before. The Emperor had them on display and sometimes they were used in the arenas. This king cobra however was a one of a kind, a monster and probably worshipped as a god by these jungle folk. Bargavon calculated the length of the body to be in excess of eighty feet and thicker than a man's torso. Its massive body slowly slid off the branch and out of view at the top of the waterfall.

A moment later the massive cobra hood protruded through the cascading waterfall and lowered itself into the natural pool. It swam leisurely across the small stretch of water to the sandy shore where the human built edifices of worship stood as did Bargavon and the Shaman. The giant cobra rose up to tower over them. Its eyes were solid shiny black orbs of ancient intelligence and death. Its forked tongue darted out tasting the mix of scents in the air, namely a bit of fear and a punch of adrenaline emanating from Bargavon.

This is how I die thought Bargavon, *how heroic. Too bad no one in the Empire will know that this happened. Would have made a good story. I won't even get my blade halfway to him before he's pumping enough venom into me to kill an elephant.* Bargavon simply broke into a slow smile excepting his death. Most men would have pissed themselves staring into the eyes this monster just feet away. But Bargavon wasn't most men, and anyway he stopped pissing himself in battle years ago.

Maybe I pissed myself, can't tell. I'm so drenched from this steam bath of a jungle. It was a strange feeling to finally meet something face to face that will kill him so efficiently, so quickly, so decisively that it will not even be a contest. And then, the unthinkable happened.

From the massive king cobra emanated a deep resonant voice. "Step away Shaman and let me inspect this human abomination."

It talks, and doesn't seem to like me. That's not good. Bargavon didn't move a muscle but his peripheral vision told him that Mokantai had slowly stepped back and away. The god-snake circled him, creating a ring of black serpentine death around him. He could hear the forked tongue flickering in the air, just a foot from him. His skin crawled and he resisted every instinct to jump and run as well as his combat trained reflex to fight the monster. The massive head lowered in front of Bargavon's face and its eyes, those deep pools of Black Death, locked onto his.

"There is the scent of my brother upon this ignorant flesh-encased ape from beyond the jungle. Shaman, how is this so?"

Mokantai retold the story he told to Bargavon at the foot of the temple, including the events that transpired with him, the Jaguar God and the dark warrior beyond the veil. The god-snake named Anaghandra never moved nor shifted his death gaze off Bargavon, who only could stand helplessly still in a ring of death before this magnificent beast. His mouth had gone completely dry as all the water in his body was sweating out every pore.

The deep resonant voice spoke again from the mouth of the great cobra, "You have passed through the Great Veil and returned a fragmented, broken fool, too ignorant to know the significance of your actions. You have caused havoc with your poor judgement and blundering presence. Yet, you managed to pass through the veil of the world and split yourself into two without dying in the process. Know this human, you walk now in two worlds, one of which you have not been prepared for. This cannot be changed. It seems the Jaguar God may have been amused and curious with your mystical blunderings, but I am not. Your fate is beyond my realm, as well as my concern. I am of the Earth and I serve her. Let the Celestial Sky-gods or my brother sort you out. Go, leave the jungle and tramp blindly to your destiny human. I will not help you, but I will not interfere with this." His last words were pointed toward the Shaman who was off several yards behind Bargavon. At that he turned, the wall of black smooth scales surrounding him uncoiled its encirclement and the great cobra-god Anaghandra withdrew and slid back into the pool. His great serpentine curves moved across the water and under the waterfall out of sight.

A sudden hand clasped on his shoulder sending Bargavon jumping straight into the air, his reflexes finally given the opportunity of release.

"Come, we are almost halfway to the village. I need you out of the jungle before the chief returns. Even Anaghandra doesn't want you here. I thought he might give us some council, some insight since you went beyond the Veil, but another answer may present itself." Bargavon turned and followed him down the path.

"What is the solution for this so-called fracture or split of my spirit as you put it. I feel like I am in one piece barring the cuts and burn."

"You're broken. Any Shaman or priest can see that. You definitely broke some ritualistic protocols. Usually, the apprentice Shamans enter the underworld and are met by and attended to by their spirit animal. You opened up a rift into a dark, unresolved part of yourself. Normally the Shaman Initiate returns to this world whole and transformed. I have never seen one return carrying with them the actual physical wounds suffered from beyond the Veil. You have a lot of work to do to resolve this problem and with no education and experience in which to properly deal with it. This is further complicated by the fact you now have the power to walk between the worlds and have an aspect of yourself prowling there. I can say with some authority the Jaguar God was amused at the novelty of your situation. Who knows, he may follow your folly with interest." He finished and reached for another flask in his bag and began to drink it.

"Wouldn't mind another drink," stated Bargavon still quite parched.

The Shaman gave him a sidelong glance "No. This IS jungle wine and I deserve a flask after having to deal with you. Here, you drink this, it will help with the hangover from the Shamanic elixir."

He reached into the bag and pulled out another gourd. Bargavon pulled out the stopper and drank from it. It was plain water and it was as refreshing as any Medregorian vintage he had ever drunk.

The two men traveled perhaps another hour following Bargavon's previous swerving track along the jungle path until they reached a village. He noted the jaguar tracks started right at the edge of the wood-line.

Quite strange. Is the Shaman a skin changer; after Jaguar and Cobra gods, why not? He thought.

It was a primitive tribal village of small wood and mud huts in a clearing. The huts were elevated off the ground by thick poles. Their roofs were thickly thatched with dried palm fronds. Wooden ladders reached the entrances which were essentially nothing more than covered platforms. A group of about twenty women and three young men were in the center of the village around a smoking fire. They were essentially naked except for loincloths. They were brown in color with straight black hair, the men wore theirs close-cropped and shaved in a strange pattern, the women loose and long. All had various tattoos on their bodies and faces, mostly lines or swirling patterns.

One of the women caught his eye, a young busty beauty that had all the right womanly curves that men of any culture would find appealing. This jogged his fuzzy memory of the previous day's events. Was that the dark haired beauty he remembered?

As if to confirm his thought, Mokantai nodded to her "Kalyani, the chief's daughter….and your death sentence should Ukko get here before you leave."

The woman was helping to pile wood upon the fire; others were squatting down working with clay pots or sorting through what looked like small piles of flowers, fruits, plants and other assembled materials. A few were placing the bodies of dead tribesmen on reed mats. Another man brought some drums down from one of the huts and an elderly woman appeared to be stirring a large clay pot as another broke off small pieces of leaves, crumbled them in her hands and dropped them in the pot. Organizing the whole affair was a robust elderly man, a tribal elder too old to make the far off journey with the chief.

"They are preparing a funeral ceremony for their dead that they suffered from the Aru attack, which you helped to repel. They prepare their dead and burn their bodies. As for the Aru, they drag them off into the jungle and dump them on ant piles. Despite your crazy antics after drinking the elixir, you most likely saved this village from cannibalism by the Aru. At least you did one honorable act. Come I will take you to my hut. It is not too far although maybe your addled brain will remember pilfering the elixir from it. We will gather a few things and then I can take you to the coast."

Mokantai and Bargavon headed into the village clearing. The villagers all stopped to stare at the Shaman returning with the crazy foreigner that had caused so much mayhem. Mokantai rattled off something in their tongue in his raspy voice that seemed to ease the tense postures by what few men remained. The frozen stares also melted away, although several women herded the young up the ladders into the elevated huts anyway, looking back with suspicion. They moved among the villagers who went back to work, but their attention was on the mail clad warrior. Mokantai continued to talk in a tone that seemed calm and reassuring to the villagers and his body language and gestures seemed to mirror this.

A brown hand grabbed at Bargavon's arm. He turned to see Kalyani, the chief's daughter smiling at him. Behind her a couple younger women were laughing. She was wearing only a small loincloth and a suggestive smile. In her other hand she was offering a gourd with a dark liquid in it. Bargavon was about to take it, *that and I'll take her again too.* A scolding tone came from the Shaman and Kalyani dropped back pouting.

"Problem Shaman?" inquired Bargavon looking back at the dark beauty he desired to spend a bit more time with.

"She thinks you have come back to court her. She was offering you some jungle wine. A couple draughts of that and you two will be wrecking a few reed mats in her hut, she'll then expect a courtship for marriage. You of course wouldn't get to the second part because Ukko's hut is burned down and you slept with his daughter. You're a walking dead man, Medregorian. Further delay of your departure puts you that much closer to your inevitable death by an enraged chief and father. We're here."

They had stopped at one of the smaller huts and Bargavon followed the Shaman up the crude ladder. "I thought you were an important man, why do you have one of the smaller huts, Shaman?" said Bargavon looking around the cramped dwelling.

The Shaman looked at him sourly, "You Medregorians are ignorant. This dwelling has all I need. A place to sleep and a place for storage and preparation of my medicines. I have heard you Medregorians recreate whole mountains out of rock to serve as a dwelling for just one family, an opulent waste."

Bargavon knew he meant the grand palace of the Royal family and he was partially right. He decided not to ask any more questions and looked about. Mokantai slept on a simple reed mat with a skull for a pillow. Bargavon's eyes rested there a moment to consider its actual comfort. Mokantai caught the stare.

"It is the skull of my master. When a Shaman dies he bequeaths his skull to the Shaman he apprenticed so he can relay wisdom from beyond the veil into his dreams." Bargavon wanted to know more but decided to keep quiet and just nodded. He was still trying wrap his mind about traveling into some sort of dream world, jaguar and snake gods and supposedly wreaking himself into parts.

There was a low crude table set with hollowed-out gourds, clay flasks, carved wooden bowls and cups, and small wooden baskets. They held everything from dried herbs and flowers, ground up powders, seashells, feathers, animal skins, bones, fungus and mushrooms, leaves of all sorts, some hanging to dry and some soaking in a large bowl of water. He had a couple of stone pestles and mortars for grinding, as well as a collection of simple tools made of flint, bone, wood, jade or obsidian. He was shuffling through the collection of these things and passed Bargavon a bowl into which he had poured a light red sweet smelling liquid.

"Drink it. It's Kanja juice. It will speed up your healing and help you rid yourself of the last effects of that elixir. It will perk you up too"

Bargavon did not hesitate. The juice was incredibly sweet and tasted of citrus, cane sugar and berries with a sharp bitter finish. He drank it all and within moments felt better, much better in fact.

"I put dried coca leaf in it. It will keep your energy up to get you to the coast," said the Shaman stuffing some dried strips of meat and another stoppered water gourd in a small sack.

They had just left the hut and descended the ladder when some shouts and whistles came from some of the villagers. The Shaman froze for a moment looking toward the edge of the jungle where they had come not more than twenty minutes before. Bargavon did not even have to ask for he could see the concern on the Shaman's face.

"They are welcoming the Chief back to the village. I misjudged his arrival."

Bargavon saw some of the children running to the jungle edge as a few tribal warriors appeared from the dark foliage. Naked, except for a loincloth, body paint and most carrying spears, or sharpened obsidian stone axes. More villagers began to shout and run to the homecoming of their warriors. A lot had happened during the few days they were gone.

The chief appeared with the bulk of his warriors. A good score of men armed with bows, spears, clubs and axes. Ukko was the tallest and biggest, nearly six feet in height and colored with multiple hues of inked tattoos. If that wasn't enough to indicate he was the chief, the headdress of feathers and the obsidian and jade necklace would signal him as the most important man present. At first, he seemed joyous at seeing his people, but a few seconds of bad news and finger pointing to his burnt dwelling, to his daughter and finally toward Bargavon's direction transformed that happiness, to shock and then a flash of anger. His eyes bulged and took on a crazed expression. He was looking directly at Bargavon.

Bargavon stood and met the chief's molten stare. He returned it with cold eyes of a trained killer. "Too late Shaman, my destiny ends here. My regards to your cat and snake gods, feel free to lump my remains on their altars….along with Ukko and most of his men." His hand calmly rested on the pommel of his sword.

Chief Ukko yelled out a challenge to Bargavon and thrust his club into the air, with his other hand he drew from a thick thong around his waist an obsidian dagger, razor sharp. Bargavon unsheathed his sword and slowly started forward, his cold eyes fixed on Ukko. Mokantai did not interfere. This was the game of warriors, not priests or Shamans or men of wisdom. He had seen this many times. His duty came after the consequences of men's bravado and recklessness. Both warriors approached each other, weapons out. The rest of the villagers moved away in a large arc and the warriors began to form a large circle near the center with the rest of villagers moved safely behind them.

The two combatants were only paces away from each other when shrieks from the other end of the village center caused both warriors to stop abruptly. Bargavon turned around to see with relief something quite unexpected. A full squad of Imperial Marines broke through the jungle greenery from the edge of the village. Their appearance caused a wave of panic from the villagers, who ran behind their warriors. The warriors quickly withdrew and closed ranks around their chief. Spears, knives, wooden clubs and a few short bows were drawn up and both sides faced off just 20 paces apart.

"Captain Bargavon, you're alive!" shouted the Imperial commander his face a broad smile partially concealed by the face guards of his steel helm. The marines were quite aware they were outnumbered three to one, but Imperial marines were the ultimate fighting force in the known world. Highly trained, well-armed, and armored, they were more than a match for the tribesmen. Bargavon withdrew slowly stepping backward to the marines, never taking his eyes off the chief, nor did the chief take his eyes of Bargavon. A collective breath was held by all for a few brief moments.

It was arrows whistling out from the jungle foliage that initiated the battle. There was some initial confusion on both sides as arrows and spears fell about them. The chief of the rival Aru tribe had chosen this moment to exact revenge for the killing of his son, whom Bargavon apparently slew with the village tribesmen. A third band of warriors burst forth into the clearing, mostly falling on Chief Ukko's warriors, but some also chose the foreign invaders to fight against as well. A well-placed arrow shot went right through the neck of a marine next to Bargavon. The arrow punctured an artery spraying a stream of blood. Bargavon quickly reached down and took up the shield from the dying marine's arm. Tribesmen were everywhere, and the marines did not distinguish between them while they landed sword blows and spear thrusts. These were Imperial marines and they fought in close formation. Their armor and shields gave them superior protection; their years of training kept them from being flanked or overexposed.

Wooden spears bent and snapped against steel shields and helms. Clubs and sharpened obsidian blades could not penetrate the marines' armor well and inflicted only cuts on exposed flesh. A stab of sharp pain from a spear thrust from a tribesmen brought Bargavon's attention to his left. His mail snapped the point of the spear but the impact into his flank was quite painful. He spun from the blow and landed a backhand slash into the exposed chest of the tribesman creating a gaping wound and a shower of blood. The marine commander next to him blocked a spear thrust with his shield and drove his sword through the torso of his attacker.

"Drawback!" ordered the commander as the marine unit withdrew in good order, pulling themselves to the edge of the fighting and out of the center of the village. The two rival tribes were upon each other with vicious intensity and bloodlust. Bargavon could see Chief Ukko cave in the skull of an opponent with his club and looked up scanning the melee. He spied the Medregorians withdrawing from the fray and Bargavon could see the frustration in his eyes. He wanted Bargavon but he and his men were too busy fighting their rivals.

The Medregorians quickly withdrew from the village. This was not their fight and they had found what they came looking for. Bargavon had been found and was safe. The marines suffered only one dead from the initial attack and a few more needed binding of stab wounds upon exposed flesh. With haste they moved up the trail, the commander turned to Bargavon, "Glad to see you're alive. Those savages looked to be ready to eat you."

"Yes, well, I am glad you arrived when you did. I think that the second group was the actual cannibals. I did, however, make the village chief rather angry for sleeping with his daughter and burning his hut down," replied Bargavon. The commander laughed. Bargavon learned they were only an hour march to the coast and would reach it hopefully by late afternoon. He was told that there were two war galleys on the beach combing the coast for survivors. It appeared there was a sudden storm a few days ago that hit the fleet. One galley was sunk and the one he was on had smashed against the rocks.

Along the way, Bargavon noticed a spotted jaguar at times trailing them. No one else noted it except him and it mostly stayed out of sight. He normally would have found it strange that it would be tracking such a large body of men, but if Mokantai the Shaman was correct, his life might not be normal anymore.

The jungle suddenly gave way to a wide stretch of beach. Two war galleys were pulled up onto the beach. Waiting there at the edge of the jungle too was Mokantai the Shaman.

I am no longer surprised at the strangeness of this jungle.

Bargavon told the marines to lower their weapons, that this tribesman was a friend. They did so and began to file off toward the ships.

"I am not even going to ask how you got here ahead of us, Shaman, but I am sure some of your jungle magic was involved. Even my people have shapeshifters and skin changers in our myths and tales," stated Bargavon.

"Are you implying I turned myself into a jaguar?" smiled the Shaman dryly, feigning disbelief at the accusation.

"I do hope your villagers live, especially Kalyani. I wouldn't mind seeing her again."

"When I left, Chief Ukko was victorious and was busy killing the rest of the fleeing cannibals. Kalyani and the others are safe. You killed one of the Aru's strongest warriors and after that their fighting spirit began to crumble. Again, you have unwittingly saved that village. I meant to give you this back at the village before the battle. I thought we would have time to talk, but I see that opportunity is not available." Mokantai placed a small carved stone in the shape of a jaguar into Bargavon's hand. It was tied to a length of tough fibrous band in the form of a necklace. "What is it?" said Bargavon looking over the smoothly polished obsidian.

"It is a totem of the Jaguar God. He seems to be curious about you. Wear it when you sleep at night."

"Will it guide me or protect me?" inquired Bargavon fingering the totem

"Bah! No, you ignorant Medregorian, it will help me find you beyond the Veil to help guide you. Despite your careless foray into a world you do not understand, I am curious to see if you make it through, perhaps give you some guidance when I can."

"That is kind of you, Shaman."

"Kindness! Oh no, you misunderstand. The Jaguar God told me too."

Bargavon laughed at the sour expression upon the Shaman's face. "Give your Jaguar and Cobra gods my regards. I am glad they decided not to eat me."

"Perhaps you can give them your regards yourself when you see them warrior. You now walk between both worlds. There is no turning back now." At that Mokantai, Shaman of the jungle tribes, turned and melded into the dark gloom of the jungle.

Commander Branta, leader of the marine unit was a few paces off. "We're ready to depart captain."

Bargavon stared into the jungle gloom a bit longer trying to wrap his mind about what the Shaman said, and all that had transpired in the last couple days. There was still an un-realness to it all and his rational mind was still working the all the fragments into a plausible story. Bargavon decided he would keep most of his experiences in the jungle to himself. Talking snake gods, jaguar gods, dark shadow warriors and passing into other realms of existence play well with the priesthood, but not with the military.

Chapter 3

Homecoming

The sounds of horns were recalling search parties along the coast back to the waiting Imperial war galleys. Across the beach was strewn the wreckage of the galley that carried him. Splintered timber planks, some oars, the shredded sail was stretched across yards of sand held down by the broken mast and other debris. Bargavon remembered now, the galley was driven up against a rocky peninsula. He could see just a couple hundred yards out that most of the ship was smashed there. He could see part of the hull wedged into the rock, incoming waves smashed into it roughly doing their best to dislodge it. The surf brought some of the debris to the beach where he believed he washed up.

"Were there any other survivors?" inquired Bargavon taking in the scene of destruction."

"A handful only, the rocks and sharks got most of them. One of the men saw you make it to the beach and told us it was you. We were compelled to send out search parties. It would be a terrible loss and a morale killer to the troops if you were lost," said commander Branta, waving in a squad of men near the jungle. "It is a miracle you survived in the jungle, Captain Bargavon. Those jungles are filled with great, man eating cats and headhunting tribes."

"You did well, commander and thank you." Bargavon's eyes scanned the dense line of steamy jungle beyond the ribbon of sand looking back for something he was not sure of, perhaps a jaguar or perhaps a dark warrior who looked like him. If they were there, neither showed themselves.

Aboard the ship he was given food and drink. His wound attended to by an Imperial navy healer who remarked at the healing of his wounds given how recent it was. "I am going to leave these dressings on, I am not sure what the poultices or pastes were applied, but whoever put them on did a fine job. I'll take another look tomorrow."

The ship captain approached Bargavon. "It would be an honor to have you with us for our return to Kathvitora. It is not every ship captain lucky enough to share the same deck with the 'Hero of Tondra Pass'."

Bargavon looked over the rail as they rowed past the smashed and twisted hull of the previous galley he was on. "Not so sure the last captain would share your sentiments."

The trip to Kathvitora, capital of the Medregorian Empire would take over a week. Their ship was part of an armada returning from a campaign against the rebellious colony of Adrar at the far western edge of the empire commonly called the Azillon Coast.

The first night while sleeping above deck in the warm Arysissar Sea air, he had an interesting dream. He awoke from his sleep and before him was a vast curtain. A gossamer type veil of spectral grey light. It was not very wide, perhaps a narrow opening in an otherwise pitch-black plane, but the height of it rose far up beyond vision. He stepped forward and passed through this veil. Wisps of ephemeral sheets of grey light wafted away from him as if passing through smoke and only the faintest of silk-like sensation caressed his skin. Past this curtain he entered a void. A rich textured vastness of black that seemed both empty and yet rich in texture in a rather unearthly presentation. He was aware of a presence behind him that made his hair upon his neck stand up. He turned to see the glowing yellow eyes of a large cat, a large black jaguar that emerged out of the darkness behind him. It startled him, and he began to run into the void of nothingness, the veil dropping quickly out of view into the textured gloom. The jaguar trailed him and then ran to first one side and then another as if driving him toward some unseen destination in the darkness. Bargavon then woke to the early morning sun warm upon his face. He was on a deck of the Medregorian galley and all seemed as it should.

The next night found him again passing through the gossamer like veil and into a textured black void. He was aware of a presence, it felt like the Jaguar God, if that really was what the large black cat was, but it did not show itself. He felt a magnetic pull within, a tug like sensation at his solar plexus. He allowed his movement toward where the sensation led, gradually he noticed scenery taking shape about him. A small child with dark hair was squatting down, his back was to Bargavon but it seemed to be doing something, holding something and rocking slowly back and forth. In the low light of the gloom dark figures stirred, they appeared tall, formal and imposing. As they approached the small child in a semicircle, Bargavon could see wickedness and cruelty upon their faces, their gaze directed at the child. They carried implements of punishment in their hands, sticks, switches and horse crops. It was obvious they meant to hurt the small boy.

Bargavon would not let that happen. He looked down to see Mokantai was correct in how Bargavon viewed himself. He was beyond the veil, but here was not the ephemeral translucent flowing images as presented in the religious texts

41

of the world beyond. It had a very real solidness to it. Upon him was steel mail, his sword and dagger were upon him, as were his leg and arm greaves of steel and leather. He started toward the ring of evil men drawing out his sword, but suddenly out of the darkness came a growl which froze him in his tracks. Silently, the great black cat appeared and put himself between Bargavon and the ring of men.

Bargavon thought to try to fight through the cat, god or not but something within the glowing eyes gave him pause. It was at that moment Bargavon's eyes caught something new emerging from the gloom, this time just behind the small boy. It was the Dark Warrior, or his fractured self if Mokantai was to be believed. It was an exact black silhouette of himself except for the narrowed red eyes and as it opened its mouth in a raspy hiss, he could see the fang like teeth of a predator. The child seemed unaware of all that was transpiring about him as the dark one stepped past him toward the enclosing circle of the tall cruel men. It drew forth both sword and ax and issued forth a distorted growl of rage. Wisps of dull red fire seemed to emanate off his body.

The tall cruel men attempted to get past the dark warrior, but his skill in arms and utter volcanic violence ripped through their number. His blade and ax struck true. The men shattered into dust with each strike. Their own blows fell upon the dark warrior who seemed to feel nothing. Within moments it was over. Only the dark warrior and the child remained, he scanned about and then bent down in a cloak of darkness enveloping the boy. All was dark.

When Bargavon awoke, it was dawn aboard the Medregorian ship sailing across the familiar Arysissar waters. He had questions; why did the Jaguar God want him to see the battle between the men and the Dark Warrior? Why did he prevent him from getting involved? Who or what was the small boy and why was the Dark Warrior protecting him? He fingered the jaguar totem about his neck wondering if he would ever have dreamless sleep or even pleasant dreams again.

It seemed from then on, each night Bargavon would awaken in his sleep and find himself passing through the Veil into the Dream World or whatever the place was removed from the normality of physical reality. Most nights he seemed to wander in the gloom, sometimes aware of presences near him, faint voices or sounds. Occasionally, we could glimpse faint images or scenes. It was if he was learning how to perceive or interact in the environment. One thing was becoming clear to him. Once passing through the Veil, any illusion of a dream like experience was increasingly replaced with a growing awareness and clarity of thought and action to the point that it took on a more realness than his waking state.

The ship arrived at Kathvitora, the great capital of the Medregorian Empire. Bargavon looked out at the vast naval yards of the Imperial fleet in port. Scores of war galleys and troop transports were docked and the incoming armada was further adding to their ranks. These ships along with many more merchant ships and fishing boats spread in a forest of masts and sails along the great crescent bay that lay before Kathvitora. The docks were crawling with workers as well as disembarking marines and sailors. Throngs of citizens also packed themselves in along the streets leading to and from the docks hailing their returning warriors and sailors for it was a crushing victory of the Great Medregorian Empire against the upstart colony of Adrar.

The ship was docked and Bargavon walked down the gangplank onto the crowded dock and up toward the crowded streets of Kathvitora. The streets were of cobblestone and the buildings made of stone, whitewashed and bright in the sun with splashes of color from many hues flowers hanging from balconies or flowered vines draping the sides of buildings. The roofs were of terracotta tile and most buildings stood two or more stories high, balconies were common. The warm temperate climate made for comfortable work, recreational and social activities outside on these balconies, terraces and courtyards.

He made his way through several winding streets that gradually rose uphill to his home. It was a three-story home that had a balcony overlooking the wide crescent bay dotted with ships. It was relatively spacious and quite well appointed even for a captain. Bargavon was a career officer and had been in the service since he was a conscript at age eleven. Twenty years of service, the last seven as captain. He had attained respect and honor through several campaigns distinguishing himself through bravery, cunning, and above all a legendary kill total. All this afforded him wealth, abundance and favor with the generals and even some of the nobles. Krin was there waiting for him as he opened the dark lacquered double door entrance. There was a smile on her fine Nordic face upon seeing Bargavon.

"Captain, I see you have returned safely from the campaign, I saw the vanguard of the fleet a few hours ago and made sure everything was ready upon your return."

Bargavon could see Krin, was indeed ready for his return. She wore only a fine white silk robe half falling off her shoulder revealing a provocative glimpse at the womanly curves underneath. Her long hair fell down her back like a blonde waterfall and she smelled of sandalwood and spices.

He embraced her instantly crushing her beautiful frame against his. Their lips met, and his powerful hands lifted her up and pressed her against the doorframe. Her hands gripped at the hardened muscles of his neck, back and shoulders. After a few moments she pulled away reluctantly.

"You smell of salt, sweat, leather and ship stink. Let's get you into a bath and scrub that sun-bronzed frame of yours." Her suggestive smile indicated it was more than just a bath and like most returns, Bargavon and Krin spent a few hours enjoying each other. Krin was a lusty slave and could more than match Bargavon's sexual appetites. Bargavon agreed with a simple nod and lowered her gently to the ground.

"I'll get the bath ready while you catch up with Rhiavar. He's in the courtyard. Then we'll get you settled in." Her smile and eyes burned sensually into him.

Bargavon entered the sunlit courtyard and found his father Rhiavar tending the plants that grew there. He enjoyed working in the courtyard, a work habit of years tending the vineyards on their farm in Copra. "Greetings father, I am home." Declared Bargavon

The older man turned slowly and wiped off the dirt from his hands. A smile crept across his weathered face and he hobbled across the cobblestone arms wide. They embraced warmly and Bargavon helped him to a stone bench in the shade under the overhang. Krin had come back from lighting a fire to heat the bath. She had brought them both cups of wine and sat down near them with a cup of her own.

"How are you feeling, father? I see you are keeping busy. Has Krin been taking good care of you?" asked Bargavon taking a wine cup from Krin and giving it to his father.

"Oh I have been keeping in shape fighting off all those hound dogs that keep baying after Krin."

"Don't listen to him," laughed Krin "Whenever some man approaches me on the street and gets a little too friendly your father here says (mocking Rhiavar's voice) 'Oh, you must be friends with my son Captain Bargavon, this is his woman Krin, ...I didn't catch your name.' and then they hastily excuse themselves or say that they mistook me for someone else."

Bargavon laughed. That was just like his father, bursting with pride for his son and making sure his reputation and property were safe and secure. Bargavon's reputation as a hero was well known, but so were many tales of his cold ruthlessness against enemies, and no one wanted to be his enemy.

"You been going easy on our guests while I was away?" said Bargavon looking over at the Yendessi game boards set up on a nearby table. While on tours of duty Bargavon's fellow officers that remained at the city garrison would stop by the house to check up on things. His father was an avid Yendessi player and would always challenge them to a friendly game. And by friendly game, that meant some coppers or silvers were on the line. Rhiavar was an excellent player, but always acted as though he just dabbled a bit. After a few house visits the officers soon learned defeat by a master and so they quickly learned to just wager in a few coppers before they are drained of all their drinking funds.

Rhiavar chuckled, "Oh your friends humor me a bit. Fine fellows all of them." His eyes twinkled mischievously.

Krin set her cup down, "Ugh, you should see the spectacle, he acts like an innocent child and I think he sets the pieces up wrong on purpose so that your friends have to correct them before they play. He lets them beat on him for a while before he turns the tables and wipes the floor with them. The whole time he giggles and says that he thinks he is getting the hang of it, the scoundrel!"

"Enough of my domestic exploits. Tell me about the campaign! I want to hear it all!" chirped Rhiavar, his face lighting up like a child ready to hear the accounts of battle and heroism from faraway exotic lands. And so that is how the rest of the day was spent over many cups of wine, father and son catching up. Krin stayed for most of it as well while occasionally tending to her other duties and to the bath that would have to wait until evening. She too was fascinated especially with the recounting of battle. She was, after all, from a warrior people. A game of Yendessi was played between the two men with Rhiavar winning only in the last few moves by the barest of margins. Bargavon was his father's son after all when it came to game strategy and the two had traded wins and losses between them for some years.

Yendessi is a game that is played on 3 game boards simultaneously. The playing pieces are usually carved of stone or marble. Each game board has a different rule system and strategy to win. There is some minor resemblance to chess in regards to movement for two of the boards but the third also has a chance element with the use of dice. The complexity of the game requires to one to split focus on three fields of battle and that each player may only make movement on two of the three boards per turn. The more elegant version of the game has the boards stacked upon each other on trays of crystal or glass. Poor folk also play the game but often draw out the game boards in the dirt and use much simpler common materials for playing pieces.

It was early evening before Bargavon got his bath, as well as an extended period intertwined with Krin both in the bath and in the bed. Upon his comfortable bed he looked out to the sight of the Three Stallions Constellation forming in the eastern sky. Next to him lay Krin, her fantastic Northern body curled against him. Happy exhaustion and drunkenness overtook him and he began to fall asleep. *Life was good.* His eyes closed and soon he passed through a zone of twilight and before him the great gossamer curtains that lead into the world beyond.

The night's events however were in stark contrast to his homecoming. Out of the textured darkness came the Jaguar God, its glowing cat-like eyes emerged before the rest of its feline form, beautiful in its black deadly silence. By now Bargavon did not fear the creature or god if that was really what it was. It turned and gave a low growl, gliding silently through the darkness, Bargavon followed. Its intent seemed to steer or guide Bargavon toward something unknown. Although he could not see much in the dark gloom, the atmosphere impressed upon him a dismal heavy doom. An oppressive heaviness that seem to weigh him down and a scene began to form about them.

They came to a place where the land was broken and ruined, the sky a murky morass of smoke and thick grey clouds. The light itself seem grey and devoid of color making everything upon the ground take on the hues of brown or grey. The land itself seemed to be an endless tumble of rock and fields pock marked with shallow pits or dismal grey pools.

Stunted grey trees barren of leaf with twisted branches and roots occasionally rose up amongst the desolation. Crows or vultures roosted on a few of these decorating their dead branches in a macabre rendition of ornaments.

The Jaguar God led him to a small rise near one of the stunted trees and a tumble of rock. He stopped and nodded for Bargavon to walk ahead and look out upon a hollowed out natural bowl within the landscape ringed by rock. Within clumps of grey dead grass and a few fetid grey pools broke up the pattern of corpses spread over many yards of ground. At a glance, perhaps four hundred bodies but that may have been too low a count.

Bargavon looked upon them for a moment. He had walked many a field of dead and dying men after a battle and this looked no different. It was a killing field, plain and simple. There was a dirt path leading down into the field and the Jaguar God indicated with his gaze for Bargavon to descend. He did so and made his way into the corpse-strewn landscape. Upon closer inspection it began to dawn on him, these were his kills. Not just the many warriors, soldiers, rebels and barbarians he had downed in combat, but so too townsfolk and farmers, women and even some children.

War was ugly ,and the stories told back in the Empire always seemed to leave out the more unsavory parts. He was an Imperial officer, a warrior and a trained killer. This was all his personal handiwork. Many of the people he remembered killing, but a good number he did not. Events happen quickly, but sometimes the flow of time is slow, and the memory embeds in great detail. Other times the experience happens in a blink of an eye and who or what was dropped by a sword blow or spear thrust is but a blur. He walked slowly among the bodies, taking in the distorted features or faces of anguish, the hacked limbs and mortal wounds inflicted upon them, the disturbing spectacle of their last moments before death preserved it here in full gory detail.

He made his way up and out of the killing field and wearily dropped onto a rock next to a dry tree trunk that seemed to twisting itself out of the ground, as if trying to get away from the dead earth. It had only a couple branches upon its broken frame. Upon one sat a vulture, its head slunk low as if brooding over the carrion before it. Heaviness and realization fell upon Bargavon like a millstone. His life's work was laid before him, the death of all those people and for what? For the glory of great Medregor, was it worth their deaths? Next to him sat the Jaguar God, it looked out upon the blasted landscape, impassive.

There was no judgment there. Bargavon did not cry or feel sorrow, for he was trained to be what he was even though that seemed like a shallow argument to what lay before him now. Heaviness weighed upon him, and he sat there for some time. Time here beyond the Veil was irrelevant and Bargavon was not sure if he sat pondering for an hour, a day or a century. The only thing that seemed to pass was his thoughts. Those thoughts remained unbroken as he awoke to the rising sun through the doorway to the balcony and the light reflected through the golden stands of Krin's hair falling down upon his face. She smiled and bent to kiss him.

"I missed you, Bargavon."

"Good to be back." He answered, and he meant it on more than just one level.

The next few months were generally quiet throughout the Great Medregorian Empire. There were no major border incursions, no rebellious tributary states or cities, no conquests planned and the navy was doing a fine job chasing after pirates on all three seas. For Bargavon that meant only administrative meetings with his commanding officer, General Targ and daily drilling of his company at the fields. He also spent time with his own combat training and when not pushing his well-muscled body through the rigors of training he would frequent the city archive and pour over tomes and books, old maps and dusty parchments.

Often these were plans of old buildings, architecture and maps. He studied these as if he were going to build them himself. A librarian asked him once why he studied these so much when he wasn't an architect and he would answer that he wanted to know the best choke points and ambush spots to kill his enemies. That answer would bring a confused frown and he would be left alone.

Lately, however, he was more apt to read on dreams, religious and mystical texts and myths. There was little direct bearing on many of his experiences as the stories seemed covered over with allegory and he was not a theologian who could decipher such. He considered walking down to the Temple District, the Medregorians had ninety-nine gods in their pantheon and he was sure someone in the priesthood had a better grasp on such matters. He wished now Mokantai the Shaman was here. Although he barely had time to know him, the Shaman seemed genuine whereas the priests in the Kathvitora temple district may as well be fine robed swindlers for what he knew about them.

Each night his journeys beyond the Veil often led him to the field of corpses. There he would sit and contemplate the consequences of his actions. It dawned on him one night to actually reach down and feel for the Jaguar God totem about his neck and was surprised to find it was there just like in physical reality. He brought it to his face and observed the carved obsidian stone. It was an exact duplicate in every detail, just like the chainmail we wore and the sword he carried.

"Shaman, if you can hear me I seek your assistance. I am lost as to what I should do."

Bargavon didn't really think anything would happen, but within moments a spotted jaguar was moving his way along a line of rocks and down a path that led to the familiar rock he had been sitting on each night that he now referred to as his Throne of Death. This jaguar looked familiar and he knew immediately it was Mokantai. When he arrived near the Throne of Death, he transformed into the man Bargavon knew from the jungle. He appeared in every detail like the man he met in the jungle; the dark tattooed skin, the lanky sinewy build and the simple loincloth. He still carried the staff with all of its Shamanic paraphernalia hanging off it and the large leather sack was hung by a thong over his shoulder.

"I really did not think you would come," said Bargavon standing up

"I did not come at your beckoning. I decided to see how far you have come on your explorations here," replied Mokantai.

"So this is the world beyond the Veil you mentioned back in the jungle?"

"The world beyond the Veil continues on into infinity. Its' vastness and grandeur are profound and beyond understanding. But this....." Mokantai's face soured in grimace, his hands swept side to side, "this is part of your world you and others like you helped create."

"Now what do I do?"

"Your Medregorian priests ever talk of Karma?"

"Only a couple of the sects do, but they are considered strange and aberrant by the others. We have ninety-nine gods and most talk of a hell where one suffers for eternity. I am not sure I believed them. I often thought they were in some ways in league with the royalty to keep the population in check and to maintain our society."

"I have seen parts of your so-called hell. It exists only by the efforts of people like you Medregorians, who willingly feed it. Your people are not wholly to blame. Other races and peoples also feed it. It is a universal concept of fearful thoughts." Mokantai finished and peered over the rim into the depression below. His face wrinkled and he looked back at Bargavon and shook his head.

"Not sure I want to go to hell," said Bargavon glumly

"Oh you're going all right. There is no escape of this. One way or another, you're either going to suffer and burn off your debt of violence and slaughter or you are going to have to work it off."

Bargavon perked up at the sound of working it off instead of what he pictured as millennia of fiery torture at the hands of devils.

"Oh, you want to be put to work?" said Mokantai, raising his eyebrows. "It is not easy from what I hear, but you may be far more useful to yourself and others. You have the skills and background for the line of work. I do not know the way to them but perhaps the Jaguar God does." At that, Mokantai started to walk back the way he came.

Bargavon stood expecting more information, "That's it? Just drop that on me and walk away?"

Mokantai never looked back, but continued at a faster pace. "We will see what transpires. In the meantime, why don't you talk with those poor dead people in the depression. Perhaps they can enlighten you."

Chapter 4

The Story of Krin

Bargavon did have free time in addition to his other endeavors and enjoyed the company of his slave woman Krin. Slaves were taken by conquest and it was normal for Imperial Army officers to take slaves back with them from campaigns. The commanding officers were permitted to bring home slaves provided they could afford the tax on them. Slaves in Medregor were treated fairly well since owning them was an expense and the Medregorians were a 'civilized' people.

Sometimes they would be released as freemen or women due to fulfilling obligations or perhaps the owner's generosity. Slaves that worked at the oars in the galleys, or the mining operations in the mountains were another matter. They could expect a short, hard, cruel existence. These were most often defeated enemies, rebels or criminals. Being a slave in these environments was generally a hard death sentence.

Bargavon had come upon Krin in a raid beyond the Northern Marches. The barbarians had been very active that season raiding south and ended up torching a border town and winning more than a few skirmishes against the Medregorian border garrisons. Bargavon's company was sent along with several others into the North for retaliatory strikes on the barbarian villages. In one of them Bargavon came upon a chieftains' longhouse and found a beautiful North-woman ready to be ravaged by a few Medregorian troopers. She was chained near the bed and was already quite naked. She was a real northern beauty. Tall, blonde, blue-eyed and fair of skin. To the southern Medregorians, this was considered exotic. Her body showed signs of abuse, mostly scratches and bruises that were too old to be from his men. They stated she was already like that when they arrived. Bargavon ordered them out. He wanted this beauty for himself, but he could see she had already suffered at the hands of the chieftain he had just slain minutes ago. *She was probably taken in a raid from another Northman village and the chieftain here made sure she wasn't going anywhere except his bed.*

Showing pity and compassion were rare for Bargavon and this was one of only a handful of times that he allowed these premium human qualities to surface during war and conquest. Normally he just would have taken her in that state as she was. Maybe he had just done this too many times and the youthful exuberance of rape, pillage and plunder was losing its luster or maybe he was overtaken with her beauty. As he approached her she did not flinch or quiver, but stared at him with cool defiance. He brought her a flask of ale off a table and offered it to her. She took it and drank it down never breaking eye contact with Bargavon. He smiled, nodded and rummaged about finding something for her to wear. He then went back out to the chieftain's body where he found the key upon his quickly cooling corpse. Before he let her loose he pointed sternly at her and then to himself. She nodded. He was half surprised she didn't attack him or run away. Instead, she stayed close. Medregorians were not particularly tall people unlike the Northmen. Krin was at least five foot ten inches and Bargavon himself a rather tall Medregorian was only an inch taller.

When they exited the structure, she cursed the corpse of her captor in her own guttural tongue and lashed out at some of the villagers, striking more than a few of the women and kicking one of the men who was on the ground tied up under the watchful gaze of Imperial troopers. Bargavon had to physically pull her away from the northern villagers and over to his waiting horse before she could harm any more of them. She would later tell Bargavon that she was a daughter of a powerful lord far to the north of these people where the land ends and the floating islands of ice began and that she was taken in a raid by this chieftain. He was never sure this was a true story or not but she certainly was 'princess' material not only for her beauty but also her bearing and her taste.

She was brought back to Medregor and was made to wear the metal anklet of all slaves in the Empire. It was an outward sign she was a slave, but also could be used to chain them up if need be. The anklet was inscribed with the owner's name and city. He brought her back to Kathvitora and taught her to speak Medregorian and learn all the customs. He found her to be exceptionally quick at learning and took to the Medregorian way of life very well.

Bargavon never had a slave before, because he never trusted their loyalty unlike the men under his command. He took things slow with her, privately he was very kind to her despite the history of brutality he showed his enemies of either gender. There was something he felt was special about her and he decided not to abuse his authority as her master. It wasn't long before she was more than a willing companion in the bedroom and his house never looked so clean and orderly. Before he had let her in however, he had all his weapons both personal and captured trophy weapons locked in a closet of the house. He figured she might just kill him one day and he feared his elderly father who dwelt with him would be run through with a blade first. His fear of death by one of his own weapons was put to rest the day he awoke to a noise of metal grating on tile. He found her in the great room dragging a Fybsuvian bastard sword across the room to a corner. Over the fireplace, two Northman longswords were hung and a spear was leaning against a corner.

"This sword is too heavy to hang. It will be best here," stated Krin, placing it firmly with both hands in the opposite corner and then turning to smile at her decorating endeavor. How she found the key was a mystery for some time until his father Rhiavar absently remarked one day that he was the accomplice. That solidified the fact that he could place trust in her and also cemented a future of both Krin and his father as partners in crime in many other endeavors.

Bargavon could never bring himself to say he loved her, but he would tell himself he was very fond of her. Perhaps he did this more out of protection for his own feelings. Love and caring was a concept that shared a history of pain with him and we swore never to allow it to grow for it could be used against him and so he considered it a weakness to avoid. She was everything he could hope for in a companion, but he was an Imperial Army captain and that lifestyle was not conducive to families or wives. Releasing her to freedom was not an option. He was sure she would leave him and he needed someone to care for his father. He was not blind to his own selfishness of having a beauty at home to share his bed with. Bargavon supported this argument by telling himself she lived a life of luxury despite her slave status.

When he did leave for extended periods of time, she would make sure his packs and equipment were ready even though he did his pre-check lists himself thoroughly. She would give him a kiss that would melt the hide of a frost giant and tell him to "Go kill the Empire's enemies and bring me back something nice." It became their routine and he found himself actually looking for things for her while on campaign. Exotic spices, gold or silver jewelry, gems off a dead noble's crown, fine silks from the armoire of a princess in a far off city, perfume from the personal dresser from some Sultan in Opirset.

Chapter 5

The Battle Here, the Battle There

The army was arrayed along the rocks. Hidden in the deep gulches and winding rocky dry ravines was the reinforcements. It was fortunate for them for the timing of the battle allowed the Medregorians to remain sheltered from the hot sun among the deep rocky overhangs and natural shelf of the Ahrza Ridge. Even in the deep shadows the temperature was still in the high ninety degrees. Out on the sandy desert their Jassurian allies were leading the Huud this way. Bargavon could see by the dust billowing over the gentle rise of the land that they were coming.

Bargavon took a long swig from his water flask and passed it to his sergeant next to him. "Tell the men to start getting ready. Pass the word to the rest of the Army, as well as our Baasid allies."

Bargavon thought back a month ago. The Empire received word from the Sultan of Sarwarbad that the Huud were marching across the great desert and were overcoming all that stood before them. The Jassur were a desert people that populated the south coast along the Arissisar Sea and were active trading partners with the Medregorians for many years. They were one of the few relatively friendly nations in that part of the world to the Empire and so the Emperor sent a task force with a whole army group under General Targ to help defend Sarwarbad and repel the Huud.

Warfare in this region was much different than the Medregorian way. Here, the great open desert and dry barren badlands benefitted troops that were light and mobile. Cavalry of both horse and camel were necessary here. All the peoples of this expansive region fought with light cavalry, archers both on foot and mounted and light footmen armed with wide shields, javelins and spears. Heavily armed and armored units were reserved for bodyguard attachments to the nobles or leaders. In contrast the Medregorians were experts in organized close packed formations both on foot, at sea and on horse. They relied on skill of arms and superior arms and armor. Previous battles based on normal army operating procedures and formations often resulted in defeat or rout for the Medregorian army. They just could not catch or adjust to the desert warriors great battlefield agility and loose chaotic formations. The Empire decided that this region of the world was not worth the cost and so never proceeded far in their plans to conquer the region. It was better just to make them trading partners.

The Medregorians did not entirely stay out of military entanglements with the desert peoples. They eventually learned and adapted strategies and techniques that harnessed their strengths and minimized their weaknesses. This particular battle was a good example of that. General Targ convinced the Jassur to meet the Huud in open battle and draw them into the rocky badlands just east of Sawarbad where the Medregorians would be lying in wait. The many dry ravines and gulches would funnel the Huud into killing zones. To sell the trap further, Targ had placed his army not in the most obvious choke points that the Huud may be aware of but almost at the perimeters. The Medregorians prepared large painted and dyed hide or cloth screens well in advance to provide camouflage for the troops. The Huud would be almost upon them before they could realize the ruse and be at the close range needed for the Medregorians to be most effective.

Several minutes went by and suddenly banners could be seen just over the gentle rise of sand. It was the purple and gold of the Jassur. Soon, thousands of mounted fighters on horse flew past. This went on for many minutes until they thinned to just large pockets of horsemen, occasionally doubling back then thundering past toward Sawarbad.

Baragvon watched as the last rear guard crested the rise, a few hundred men riding hard. Behind them many times their number came the forward operating Huud skirmisher squadrons, both sides firing arrows from horseback into each other. The black shafts were striking into sand, beast and man alike on both sides. Again and again the Jassur dropped away drawing the Huud vanguard after them.

A few minutes more went by, and nothing. "Maybe they saw us," spoke Sergeant Kulshendra lowly.

"No. The main force is coming, listen!" hissed Bargavon his hand clenching the rock of the ledge reflexively. His body priming itself for the combat that it knew waited ahead. Warrior training was honed into his very nervous system. Imperial soldiers were trained since their early teens. War was their life. Quietly at first, but then quickly growing a steady beat of drums was heard. Deep thudding drums, perhaps hundreds of drummers announcing to the sands of the desert and all in it the Huud were coming. Louder now the drums sounded and now the sounds of strange horns added to the percussion. The horns were a whiney detuned sound, somewhat chaotic and tense.

Over the rise came the main Huud body, a massive chaotic wave of horsemen coming by at a slow trot. Their banners were of red field with the symbol of a black pyramid. The black pyramid many said was where their god-king dwelt at the source of the three rivers of Anhkedhin.

Occasionally pockets of scores of horsemen would break and gallop forward out ahead probably to relieve or support the vanguard, but the main body, unaware of the Medregorians proceeded forward as a massive wave of human and animal flesh bent on death and destruction. On they came for some time. Bargavon guessed their numbers at sixty thousand, give or take twenty thousand. Hard to determine numbers like that after a while.

"That is a lot of Huud, captain," spoke sergeant Kulshendra finishing off the water flask.

"Yes it is, sergeant, but that means we have more to kill. The desert is dry and thirsty, and we will quench her thirst with the blood of the Huud," smiled Baragvon. "Look there, I see our Baasid friends have decided to start things off."

They looked to the left and saw a cloud of dust quickly moving behind the last remnants of the Huud. These were mostly camel trains hauling the supplies as well as a rear guard force. The Baasid really looked, and fought no different than the Huud. Only the colors of their clothing and their banners of stripped blue and white indicated they were even a different force. Before the Medregorians the line of Huudish warriors and baggage handlers began to scurry and churn about. The rear guard were hastily drawing themselves up into a mass of horsemen turning to face the approaching enemy. The baggage train was in a panicked rush to get to the safety of the rocks unbeknownst to them, waited the Medregorian army.

Three hundred yards out from the ridgeline, two massed formations of cavalry charged into each other under a hail of missile fire from both sides. Next spears clashed and drove into each other in a thunderous clash of steel, hoof and flesh.

"Now!" bellowed Bargavon rising up from his crouched position. Horns winded along the ridgeline. The trap was sprung. Scores of camouflaged screens dropped away revealing thousands of Medregorian spearmen and archers lining the spine of rock jutting up from the desert sands. The baggage train and its handlers now utterly panicked caught between Baasid horsemen and an entire Medregorian army that literally materialized right in front of them.

Thousands of arrows poured out from the rocks catching the Huudish horsemen in thick packs and felling them in droves. Bargavon was the lead company and his spearmen exploded from the rock crevasses and from under the great overhangs. They shredded through the poor pack handlers, most were running, some dropped to their knees begging mercy. *Too early for that,* thought Bargavon as he removed a head from a body that got in his way. He could see the Baasid had fully engaged the Huuds and kept their cavalry relatively static allowing for the Medregorian footmen to smash into their left exposed flank.

Bargavon threw a spear into a Huud rider ten yards from him impaling him straight through and toppling him from his mount. His men smashed through the wall of horses driving sword and spear points up into close-packed bodies. It was a packed melee that the Baasid and Medregorians forced upon the Huud rear guard. These desert warriors did not have the body armor of their adversaries. They wore only light garments and perhaps wicker and camel hide shields. Some may have had metal leg greaves as well, but not many. The Medregorians, however, wore steel helm, wooden shields bossed with steel, the heavy troops wore chainmail or scale mail, the lighter troops such as the archers and scouts leather armor.

Huudish riders had already ridden away to warn the main body of a surprise attack to the rear and this was already accounted for. The rear guard had been ground down and what was left was being routed and driven into the desert. The baggage train was completely decimated. Bargavon looked about. Thousands of Medregorian soldiers were finishing off the few survivors, and the horns and signal flags were calling them back in for reforming the ranks.

The Medregorians were setting up for a counter attack. Longer pikes had been brought in for this very purpose and they were placed at ground level to not give away their presence. They knew the Huud would rush them straight on for an initial clash after softening them up with a hail of arrows. Extra Medregorian archers were added to the roster for this very reason and they were placed several ranks back to unleash an equally deadly cloud. The Baasid took up position on the far left flank anchoring the desert against a cavalry flank. They were not numerous and numbered only a few hundred at this point in the battle. The Huud gave them some worthy losses on the initial exchange noted Bargavon.

Bargavon could not wait for this next contact. This is where the battle would really be decided. More than likely the Huud would split their main body of troops into two. Half would continue the pursuit of the fleeing Jassur, and the other half would turn and deal with the Medregorians and Baasid. By now the Huud would be elongated between both sides of the battle and this is what General Targ wanted for the rest of his trap had yet to be sprung.

The Huud did not disappoint. Thundering across the sand came the great mass of horsemen, as they got close they began to veer off discharging javelins and arrows into the static Medregorian lines. Arrows and javelin shafts found their marks impaling men but so to many were they deflected from raised shield, helm or skimmed off armor at an odd angle. The Medregorians sat there taking it. They had expected this tactic and had prepared for it. Hundreds of Medregorian soldiers dropped to the ground acting as if hit by arrows or javelins, a ruse to draw the Huud in quicker to finish off the Medregorians. The Medregorians did not return fire.......yet.

"Let them think we are sitting ducks. Hold fire. Come on fuckers, bring it in closer," grimaced Bargavon. Targ had given him command of the field. It was all on him and his iron nerves. He could see the Huud sweeping back for another missile discharge. They were coming in at an angle. The line officers were looking to him for direction.

"Hold steady. Remain in formation!" bellowed Bargavon. The order kept his men exactly as before and again the Huud came charging upon them but closer and dislodged arrows into his lines. Men screamed and fell but the line held solid. Off to the far left the Baasid could not take waiting any longer and began skirmishing the Huud cavalry. *Fucking Baasid, if they weren't in this desert they would be worthless. Too fucking early, you desert dogs!* Like a great flock of birds, the Huud whirled away again to reform up a few hundred yards away. More were arriving and their numbers were swelling

"Look men! The Huud are piling on more meat on the serving platters. We will be feasting well in the desert tonight!" Bargavon called out and his men answered with great laughter and witty responses.

"Please Captain, no more. You're making me hungry!" called one.

"At least they will be providing the blood to wash it down with!" bellowed another.

"Now I'm thirsty!" called another and a roar of laughter burst from the lines.

The Huud formed up and burst forward in another wave of horse and man. Spears were lowered, javelins and bows were drawn and scimitars brandished in the hot desert sun. On they came and this time the vector was straight on. "Fire!" bellowed Bargavon quickly turning to his signalman who winded his horn indicating to the archers to open up fire. Arrows launches from over a thousand archers. Clumps of charging horses and horsemen went down plowing into the sand riddled with arrow shafts. On they came unaware that the hidden lengthened pikes were just seconds away from skewering their lines. A second volley of death sailed through the air from the archers leveling droves of Huud. On they came. At the last few seconds, three lines of Medregorians pulled up on long pikes and the Huud shattered against the wall of timber and steel death.

The terrible sounds of cracking and snapping pike hafts, the screams of impaled horses and men, the clash and thunderous crunch of living bodies slamming into each other filled the air. The ranks of Medregorian archers did not let up.

They arched their arrows high into the air to fall upon the masses of horsemen further back from the frontal carnage.

With pikes already expended into bodies of horses and men, the Medregorian footmen rushed forward. The Huud had expected to trample over the static Medregorian lines and so the mass of horsemen became congested when the pikes abruptly halted that effort. The horsemen were being slaughtered in the front ranks under a relentless assault of sword and spear. They could not maneuver and the lack of armor was their doom.

Bargavon moved into the fray and parried a scimitar blow above his head then slashed downward across the exposed leg of a horsemen coating the side of his white mount a crimson red. He turned to look to his right as a toppling horse nearly buried him under its weight, its rider skewered through by a Medregorian spear. A deep thwack noise and a scream behind him brought him around to see one of his command staff take an arrow through the back, the horse archer firing point blank behind him and a second later he too was put down with a sword thrust. Malibar, his top lieutenant was deflecting a spear from a rider, then quickly ducking low to come up and drive his sword hilt deep into Huud cavalryman. This is where battles turn from thinking strategy and initial tactics to personal combat skill and impersonal luck or fate if one believed in the gods. And so the battle turned into a maelstrom of churning Huud horsemen and Medregorian footmen. Baragvon would have preferred it this way as this allowed them all the advantages and took away the Huuds' three best qualities; speed, maneuverability and archery. This was not to be for the remainder of the battle for the Huud commander was able to sound his weirdly detuned horns that ordered his men to pull out of the fight.

Those Baasid dogs, damn them! If they would have stayed put they would have been able to pull the pincer behind the Huud keeping them right here. Fuck. Fuck. Fuck! Bargavon could see the mass of horsemen breaking free of the jaws of the Medregorian infantry. He could also clearly see the Baasid had pulled out of the battle, they had taken a beating in a stand up fight with the Huud cavalry. Between both forces lay piles of dead and dying men and horses. The sand soaked dark with blood. Bargavon was pleased that a majority of the prone bodies were not Medregorian. With the Baasid horsemen now out of the fight and his troops fully exposed the Huud would have a much easier time picking apart his troops. He would have to rely on his extra archers to hopefully hold them at bay.

"Reform the lines!" yelled Bargavon, his line officers repeating his commands, banners were waved to help reorient the men and horns were winded. A few hundred yards away the Huud had reformed. Their commander was out front, barking orders and brandishing his scimitar waving it overhead. He was dressed in splendid chainmail and he had a silvered helm trimmed in gold. His cloak was a brilliant purple and gold. *A real peacock this guy. Easier to find for me to kill him. I think Krin will find a place for that helm on the mantle.*

The Huud broke into a charge toward the Medregorian formations. *Damn all ninety-nine gods! Not enough time!* Indeed, the Huud needed little time to reform whereas the Medregorians required more to reset their orderly formations. Men scrambled to form up but too late. Scores of men fell under a barrage of arrows and javelins as the Huud unloaded and peeled back away. The familiar tactic and an effective one against foot soldiers. The Huud could end up doing this all day and grind the Medregorians down to corpses in the sand except for one thing.

The mass of Huud horsemen peeled back away from the reforming Medregorian ranks only to turn into the sudden appearance of General Targ and the remainder of the Medregorian army. A mounted force that lay hidden in the gulches until now. Over seventy-five hundred Medregorian cavalry made up of over half heavy cavalry along with the remainder of the Baasid held in reserve numbering another two thousand smashed into the unsuspecting Huud. It was a horrendous crash of flesh and steel and one could feel the ground shake. This was the second half of the trap Bargavon was waiting for and his men sold it well. He now had time to complete the plan. With the Huud engaging Targ's cavalry, Bargavon had time to reform his men into their proper anti-cavalry formations.

He looked out at the clashing cavalry battle before him. Again, the Medregorians' use of heavier arms and armor was decisive in the close hand to hand combat and the Huud were not faring well even though they outnumbered the Medregorian cavalry almost three to one. The choice of the field of battle near the Ahrza ridges helped to congest the forces that hindered the mobility of the Huud. Their losses were piling up faster than the Medregorians and their commander ordered a retreat. The Huud broke from the fray and would have headed out to the safety of the desert if it wasn't for the encircling wall of footmen who commanded the summits of the dunes that spilled down toward the Ahrza ridgeline. Medregorian archers opened up at two hundred yards and kept up fire until the horseman made it to the front ranks. The desert sands were beginning to embrace more dead and dying bodies fitted with arrows. The Huud made a desperate charge to escape. It was a long front and through the empty gaps they streamed. The gaps allowed for killing channels by archers that had prepared for this. Those that risked the set spears of the infantry fared worse and those of the rear of the body of horsemen were being chased down by the Baasid and Medregorian light cavalry. It was a killing field after that.

It was late in the day after the battle. Wounded and surrendered Huud warriors were taken prisoner and the spoils of war were being divided up between the winning factions. Bargavon personally searched the battlefield for the body of the commander wearing the silvered helm. He was not part of the prisoners and no one noted his passing of those that broke the encirclement. *Too bad, it would have been a great piece of loot.* His path took him among the Baasid who had fallen upon much of the supply train wreckage. The Medregorians were well supplied leading up to the battle but less could be said for their allies. The Baasid fell upon the Huud supply train wreckage like locusts.

A disturbance caught his eye among the rocks. It was the cowering form of a Huud camel drover. Protecting him was a mangy dog. Surely the drover's companion animal that accompanied him across the desert. Several Baasid were harrying the defenseless man and his faithful dog. Bargavon's grasp of the desert folks' language was basic but he could tell the drover was pleading for his life and asking them to spare his dog. The Baasid said they were going to eat his dog for dinner and sell the man into slavery. *Probably true on both accounts.* The drover was an older man and surely was not a threat to anyone. Left alone, he probably would offer his services as animal handler or camp worker. The harassment was not necessary, just the normal cruelty of one group of people dishing it up to another but he found the eating of dogs abhorred and so decided to stop the drama.

"Leave him be. There is more food, wine and equipment scattered across the battlefield and he is not worth the trouble." Spoke Bargavon loudly in his best desert dialect as he strode toward the group. They turned and appeared to understand him and most stepped back but one with a bow raised it and knocked an arrow aiming at the dog.

"I said leave it!" commanded Bargavon, this time with menace. The Baasid archer just made a sour face lowered the bow, but then quickly raised it and feathered the dog solidly and just as quickly feathered another through the heart of the old drover. A couple cheers and cackle of laughter erupted from the small group. The dog was down but not dead, but the old drover was.

Bargavon was the second in command after General Targ and the Baasid were to be taking their orders from the Medregorian commanders. The Baasid obviously thought otherwise a good deal of the time. Bargavon would make sure they knew who was really the master of the field this day and apparently his reputation had not been heard among the desert folk. He would quickly change that. Killing in battle was one thing. Killing for the sake of sport because something was weaker had always bothered him. Bargavon was good at killing and apparently the Baasid had not had enough this day. Bargavon would be the deliverer of more death then. *So be it.*

He strode quickly through the group pushing two of them out of his way. The archer stood tall and proud. "This is between desert people. You are a foreigner."

"Understood." was all Bargavon uttered as his sword left the scabbard in one smooth stroke and less than a second cut the head off the archer before it could register surprise on its bearded face. He immediately turned expecting the Baasid to jump him and he was not disappointed. Three of the seven did draw their scimitars and ran at him. He parried and dodged their blows. They were not particularly skilled thought Bargavon, no wonder they took a beating from the Huud today. *Archery may be another matter*. He decided to end it quickly to bring his point home to the Baasid that Medregorians were superior in combat and that orders not followed may result in death. The second met his end with half his skull shaved off. *A helmet might have prevented that*. The third drove against him in a wild flurry of slashes that ended when Bargavon snapped the man's knee backward with a kick and then as he doubled forward put a well-placed downward slash deep into his back between his ribs and into some vital organs.

A Bassid commander arrived with a couple more men. "How dare you interrupt the dealings of my people. You have no right Medregorian!" bellowed the Bassid commander.

Bargavon was no longer at a point for polite conversation. Years of warrior training stoked the primal killing mechanism within him. Bargavon approached the commander quickly but sheathed his sword. The Baasid were going to see a display of cruelty that would leave them in no doubt why the Medregorians were the dominant force in the world and why Bargavon was a known and feared commander who never shied away from getting bloody. There was cruelty, there was Imperial Medregorian cruelty and there was a personal terrible brand of cruelty that could raises its ugliness from time to time when Bargavon saw fit.

The Bassid commander thought Bargavon was going to stop short and parlay into a heated exchange but instead his nose exploded in shrapnel of cartilage and blood from a mailed fist and down he went. His men next to him found themselves in no position to help their commander as more than a few Medregorian swords were drawn out from nearby troopers who had arrived during the commotion.

The Bassid commander impacted the ground with Bargavon atop him. He was dazed and only started to struggle and kick about as Bargavon grasped the man's jaw and began yanking it from his mandibular socket. Screams of sheer terror rent the air as it took almost a half a minute for Bargavon through the efforts of his own hands to rip away most of the man's jaw from his head and smash in his nasal cavity a few times with a mailed fist. The Bassid nearby could only stare in horror at the sudden atrocity.

Bargavon got up, his victim writhed about in the sand spewing blood from a gapped cavity that was once a face. It made gurgling sounds and coughs and strange hisses because the normal apparatus for sound making was destroyed. This man would be dying in a short while and horribly so. When he looked up from his butchery, the remaining Baasid took his advice and left. His Medregorian soldiers grimly nodded and went about their business. They had seen similar acts of violence to their enemies from their commander before. They knew it had far reaching effects upon enemies. Fear Medregor but fear Captain Bargavon more.

Someone else was watching. It seemed almost like a mirage in the hot sand, but he saw a shadowy figure sitting on the corpse of a dead horse nearby. It's only other feature were the narrow red eyes of piercing intensity. He seemed to hear its grave raspy voice in his mind, *Yet another body added to our corpse field. This is what we are, what they made us to be, what we will always be, you and I. It was not always this way was it.* As the words echoed in his mind a trooper passed in front of the image and it was gone, just a dead horse upon blood soaked sand baking in the sun.

In a strange act of compassion Bargavon had the wounded dog taken to his tent. Something the Dark Warrior said triggered a fragment of memory from a long time ago and for some inexplicable reason sparked a hint of care for a mangy baggage train dog. A healer arrived to his tent, removed the arrow and tended to the wound.

"It's a deep one Captain, it went into the lower abdomen as well. I have given it the best care and medicine we have but I am not so sure about him making it."

The healer's name was Broxa, the best of four healers he had in his company. Broxa patted the dog on the head tenderly and adjusted the blankets under the animal for comfort. "Is there anything else Captain?"

"No Broxa, tend to those who need your service and then get some rest when you can. I realize your work has just begun. Thank you."

The healer exited the tent and Bargavon spent several minutes tenderly stroking the dog. "I am sure you were a brave and loyal companion to your master. I will see to your care. If men were like dogs, we would inherent a kindness, a loyalty and a nobility of bearing far beyond what we possess now. Sleep and rest brave animal."

It was near sundown when Bargavon made his way to

General Targ's tent. He was tired but buoyant. Victories tend to imbue that kind of paradoxical but satisfying feelings. He saluted the bodyguards and entered. General Targ poured them both cups of wine and set it on a table. On the table Bargavon spied the silver and gold trimmed helm of the Huud commander.

"That helm appears to be separated from its previous owner. I recognized it from the battle." indicated Bargavon taking a cup of wine from his general.

"Yes, the owner not only was separated from his precious helm, but also seemed to be separated from his body too." Smiled Targ pointed to a corner of the tent where a bearded decapitated head lay. "I present to you Sultan Warbah, previous commander of the Huud army and late son to their supposed god-king in the south."

"That's why the other force chasing the Jassur bolted after their defeat by us in the rear. I assumed the Sultan was leading the main body. With his death, the Huud routed, makes sense now." pondered Bargavon thoughtfully.

"I heard there was some trouble with the Baasid after the battle. Apparently, there was some minor trifle that ended up in a few deaths of our allies. They are our allies for now and they do have their usefulness. I am going to assume it was warranted?" queried Targ. He trusted his high captain and would not pry further.

"Yes General, it was. Sometimes people need reminding who is at the top of the command chain and sometimes the reminding needs to be effective, sometimes brutally effective." replied Bargavon scowling into his wine cup. "This is good, from home?"

"I always bring a jug of Narsandran Red as a celebratory drink. Have another cup. If not, I'll drink it all and pay the price for it tomorrow." said Targ smiling, pouring himself another cup. The two drank and talked into the night until sleep overtook the post battle high. Bargavon returned to his tent, saluted his guards and went inside. The dog was breathing in short shallow breaths on the blankets at the foot of his cot. In the dim light of the tent he could see the dog's eyes were closed but opened when he sat down next to it. He petted it slowly in long soothing strokes. The dog's breathing slowed somewhat and appeared a little calmer. He looked down at the animal. An innocent casualty of war, Bargavon had seen plenty of these, men, women, children and animals. Lots of cultures talked about their war gods and how the warriors died and arrived in an afterlife of eternal battle and eating and drinking in the halls of their gods.

That sounded like meaningless work and toil to Bargavon. He also heard of talk by the priests of those faithful that sang in a choir that exalted their god for eternity. He was not sure this was something to strive for as it seemed more like a boring tedious hell to him. He wondered if there was an afterlife for animals. He looked down at the dog. He knew it was dying and if he helped it pass on in some comfort to whatever waited it beyond the veil, well then that would be the second best thing he did today besides destroying a Huud army. The dog triggered a memory from long ago, a simpler time, a happier time in his youth before the Empire twisted him into the implement of war he was today.

Best to leave those memories lie in the past; they will no longer serve me. No place for such memories now. The wine and the day's battle were taking its toll. Sleep came upon him.

He passed through the Veil as was now commonplace, but instead of the familiar dark gloom it opened to the local battlefield at Ahrza. He could see his tent with his guards stationed outside by a low fire and his gaze swept to the multitudes of similar tents and watch fires along the Ahrza Ridge. There was movement in the periphery of his vision. His senses indicated danger and he quickly spun and drew out his sword. His reflexes narrowly caught a similar blade striking down upon him. Here in the dream twilight superimposed upon the physical world, his dark aspect, the Dark Warrior was upon him.

They fought among the corpses of both horse and man there upon a sandy dune. The ringing of their swords were silent as was their desperate combat among the few soldiers that happened to be at the watch fires no more than fifty yards away. Ghosts generally are silent to the living.

"Why are you fighting me? What have I done to you? Are we not one and the same?" bellowed Bargavon parrying away the others well placed strikes while equally trying to land the same. "Stop for two fucking minutes!"

"You attacked me first! I know what you fear. What I carry you cannot abide. You will try and kill me to bury it!" rasped the Dark Warrior striking even harder with each word. A few got past and bit into Bargavon's mail and slashed across his bare forearm and leg.

Bargavon felt the burn, the sharp pain and numbness. He felt the wetness of blood splattering down his arm and leg. *Is one supposed to feel and bleed beyond the Veil? Can I be mortally wounded and die here on this side as well? This does not feel different than in the physical world I know these wounds from him carry over.*

There was a hard-raspy laugh from the Dark Warrior as if in response to Bargavon's thoughts. "Feel me for I am your pain! I am your grief! Death and departure from me is impossible. You must face me!" roared the Dark one, his red eyes widened, and his predatory maw shown stark white against his impenetrable blackness of form.

Bargavon managed to kick him in the torso and followed up with a deep stab into the torso. He felt the tension of what may have been mail, tissue and sinew upon his blade as it sunk into the black form. It screamed out in pain and pulled back. The Dark Warrior stepped back, blood as red as Bargavon's hit the sand in streams of crimson.

"I...won't stop...we'll meet again and again until...the end." It croaked out in a hollow tinged voice. It stumbled and fell behind the corpse of a camel. Bargavon ran to where it fell but the shadow form was not to be found. It was if it disappeared into the shadows cast by fire and the sliver of moonlight upon the dune.

Bargavon looked down. He still bled profusely from wounds on his arm and leg. He felt the contrast of warm wetness of the blood and the numbing coldness of the wound. He limped up to the top of the dune, unsure of what to do. Was there aid on this side of the Veil, beyond the physical and wondered what death was like in this concept of existence. He clutched at the Jaguar totem about his neck. "Help me." Was all he could say, all he could think of. His legs started to falter a little. Bargavon looked out at the desert, a palette of muted blue and silver grey under the pale light of the moon and stars. But there on the next ridge of dunes was the Black Jaguar, sitting as if expecting him.

He stumbled down the slope and up the other dune determined to reach the Jaguar. His legs were giving way for he was losing a lot of blood. *How is this possible*? But it was and he did make it to the summit of the dune, dizziness and weakness coming upon him. The Jaguar God simply turned and led him along the ridgeline. Bargavon followed for he knew no other option. His focus narrowed to just watching himself place one foot in front of the other, barely staying upright, drops of blood pelting the soft sand between strides.

Finally, he succumbed and his numbed body collapsed into the soft night-cooled sand. He could see the Jaguar God sitting serenely a short distance away watching him and then turn its face toward a light that fell upon it from above. The Jaguar God seemed to follow a movement from behind Bargavon and then turned away slowly, looked back once to meet Bargavon's gaze and then vanish into the night over the ridgeline.

Bargavon felt hands upon him. He was gently turned over onto his back. Above him a warm golden glow flooded his vision. He could see a face, almost as if it were a golden mask of a smiling man somehow superimposed upon a smooth golden mask scintillating with varied colors changing by the second. It seemed to be in dull golden colored armor of fine fitting plates.

To either side of the golden one, visages of grim-faced men, warriors by the look of them in strange heavy gear and armor. One of them had a reddish beard and a menacing scowl upon his face sneered. "Ah, this fucking guy, seriously, this never gets easier does it?" he looked off to someone beyond Bargavon's vision. "Mine? Yeah, I got him, no issues Commander."

To the edge of his vision behind the crush of faces rose something out of the night, a monstrous blue head that could only be described as rhino-like.

It spoke in a deep bass-like voice, "What do you make of him?"

The golden-hued smiling face one replied in a voice that was both polite and pleasant, "He will fit right in. He carries the signature for sure. He's a piece of work."

"A little beat up by the looks of him," said the big blue thing.

Some laughter rippled from the grim looking men about him. One chuckled, "Hell, I looked like this after the first run today."

"That's because you're fucking careless," chided another somewhere out of sight of Bargavon.

The golden one answered the big blue one after the laughter subsided. "Not bad at all really, just superficial stuff. We'll get him in the transport and patch him up good as new......uh oh."

"What is it?" inquired the big blue rhino thing as the other men were lifting Bargavon up onto a stretcher

"He also has a signature of one still having a body in the physical world," replied the gold smiling one.

"Some people just can't wait, can they? Well, I guess it means he just gets a head start. Better keep him close with me and Big Red. He is going to need some baby-sitting and hand holding for a while. I hope he will be worth the trouble," said the Rhino like thing lumbering next to the big red bearded warrior, who carried him on the litter. He could feel them traversing an incline and a pale-yellow light fell upon him. He could vaguely see a light filled rectangular portal as his vision began to blur. His hearing was starting to dull and the voices became muffled.

"Oh, he's worth it. He looks to be a bit of a monster with some serious issues though. You know how these humans are. Mixed bag all of them. Got to take the good with the bad. This one's got some skill, but he's a bit broken," said the golden-smiling one. He seemed to be working on Bargavon's wounds with some materials he could not recognize. Whatever it was it was immediately soothing and his pain was being replaced with a soothing comfortable numbness.

The big blue rhino snorted, "He fractured a bit? Missing a piece or two?"

"Yeah, we'll see how bad it is. He should still be serviceable though."

There was no more that night, just dark dreamless sleep for once after all these months.

He awoke the next morning, his body stiff and aching in every muscle and joint of his body. Typical pains from yesterday's battle, but he was surprised to find no evidence from his battle with the dark one. *I was a wounded mess back on the pyramid with my first fight with the Dark Warrior. Did those other guys that found me heal me on that side? Who were those guys?* His head throbbed from too much of the General's wine and he slowly pieced together last night's activities beyond the Veil. He had a lot of questions, but they would have to wait until tonight.

He looked down, the dog had climbed up on his lap in the middle of the night and died. A wave of sadness came upon him. It reminded him of a simpler time when he use to help a friend find and take care of injured animals. Those memories started to come up and express themselves, but he stifled it and pushed it back down deep in the recesses of his mind and body. He had no time for such memories or feelings. He was a warrior and a high captain of the Imperial Medregorian Army with many responsibilities today. There was no room for sentiments and soft emotions. Not anymore and not for a long time. He personally buried the dog and then went about his business of commanding Medregorian soldiers and meeting his command staff to work through the remains on the battlefield.

Over the next few days he and the army moved into temporary barracks within the city of Sawarbad. His activity became the mundane management of patrols, reports and inspections. The Huud were decimated and only a small part of their original invading army made it back out into the empty vastness of the desert.

Bargavon's nightly sojourns, however, took a strange turn. For two nights he slept a dreamless sleep. No activity or memories of passing beyond the Veil. It was if it was over and part of him sighed with relief, while a deeper part of him seemed to miss the dark adventure and wonder of it all.

Everything changed however on the third night. He awoke seeing the Veil pass by him rapidly and he felt as if a force was carrying him at great speed through the darkness until he arrived at a wooden dock dimly lit by oil lanterns. His eyes followed a wooden ramp that led up to the side of a ship. It appeared to be a troop transport of some kind. Out of the gloom came a man in peculiar heavy armor he had never seen before. Heavy torso plate dull green in color with paint chipped away revealing the steel gray beneath. His muscular arms were bare and his pants were baggy with many sewed on pouches. Odd looking arm and leg greaves, the color of his torso armor, were strapped on him. He wore no helm but instead a black cloth cap fit snug upon his head. His face was of a grizzled veteran with hard lines. He had a short dark peppery grey beard and his eyes shown hard and black. He carried a strange black crossbow that hung from a strap around his neck.

Bargavon slowly drew his longsword and reached back for his ax with his left. The armor looked strong on this individual and having the ax in his left may provide him with another option to puncture through it or within the exposed openings. He looked down, as always his chainmail hauberk was upon him as were his own steel arm and leg greaves. He cautiously moved forward. The warrior upon the ramp continued his descent and made it to the dock, his eyes were trained on Bargavon's. The warrior spread his leg apart a bit, his arms moved to rest upon the weapon slung before him and his head tilted back a little eyeing Bargavon with a casualness that projected a calm assuredness. He did not project the image of an imminent attack, so Bargavon lowered his weapons to his side.

"The name's Gage. I am here to ease you into the Company. You can be at ease warrior."

"I don't know what I am doing here. I know I'm beyond the Veil, but how I got here is a mystery," replied Bargavon realizing there was no immediate danger from the individual named Gage. He re-sheathed his sword and slung his ax back over his shoulder.

"You can thank Jaguar God for that. He whisked you out here," replied Gage raising his hand in a wave and looking past Bargavon to something in the darkness. "We got 'em, all's good Big Cat."

Bargavon turned around to see glowing yellow eyes off in the dark gloom turn and disappear soundlessly. He turned back to Gage perplexed.

"Yeah, Jaguar God, huh?" shrugged Gage "I don't know, those gods always seem to have some sort of angle or game going on. Beats me, I'm just a grunt like you. Don't try and think about it all too much or your mind will cave in. It's kind of a lot for a new guy and besides, I heard you still got a body back in the physical. Easy for you to get all twisted up trying to sort it all out."

A deep horn sounded up past the ramp. Gage turned and waved to someone Bargavon could not see at the top. "Let's go, we got a run to do. We'll brief you on the way."

Bargavon had a hundred questions needing immediate answer but followed Gage up the ramp. Considering he seemed to be placed here purposefully and he hadn't really met anyone besides the Shaman, the Dark One, the Jaguar God and corpses of his past kills, all of which weren't particularly talkative. This night was becoming very interesting.

The ramp came up to an opening in the side of the great wooden-hulled ship. Inside was the cargo hold of the ship with a central aisle way and to either side benches built into the curved shape of the hull. There were racks and lockers bolted to the side along with webbing holding all manner of what he perceived as military gear, armor and armament, most of which he could not really identify.

There was a flurry of activity as about a hundred warriors were busking for combat. Warriors were the best term he could use at the moment because 'men' may not be fully accurate. At least a quarter of them were not human in appearance. Had Bargavon not been acquainted with the couple of Shamanic gods and the dark warrior he might have questioned his sanity and immediately claimed this just a nightmare from which he could not wake up.

"A little much, eh?" said Gage turning to see if Bargavon had fled back out the ramp.

"I'm good," said Bargavon simply. Over two decades of harsh Imperial training and warfare could harden one's resolve.

"We're over there. This is our squad," pointing to a cluster of seven other warriors, "and that over there is our squad leader," pointing to the big blue rhino like humanoid Bargavon remembered during his rescue in the desert a few nights previous. As if hearing Bargavon's thoughts he smiled and turned, "Yeah, Big Blue, that's what I call him too. It's funny how a description of someone becomes their name. You couldn't pronounce his given name if you tried. Humans don't have the vocal equipment."

"You read my mind?" said Bargavon taken aback.

"You're on this side of the Veil man, thoughts start to become things. They broadcast out. You will learn to shield them in no time. Our thoughts help us all communicate with each other. Did you think we all spoke the same language? It just appears to you that way. Your mind is filtering and squashing things down in this reality to what you are capable of understanding. Like this ship here," Gage reached out and pounded on a wooden timber support beam. "I bet you think this is some sort of sailing ship made of wood."

Bargavon nodded. Gage looked hard into his eyes for a moment and suddenly the surroundings looked different. The interior was a dark dull grey and metallic and many of the structures changed shape. The oil lanterns flickering lowly transformed into tubes of low red light giving everything a reddish hue. Only the warriors looked the same. Gage released his gaze and all returned to the wooden cargo hold as before. "That is how I perceive it. Who knows what it really is. Maybe we're carried in a celestial whale's belly."

A cascading of chaotic mental processing in Bargavon's mind was interrupted by a heavy slap upon his shoulder. He turned to look up at the large blue rhino thing.

"You're with my squad. You can call me 'Big Blue' if you like, everyone else does. I am your squad leader." His massive hand wrapped around Bargavon's shoulder turning him to face the rest of the squad. He began pointing to the warriors nearby busy strapping on armor and gear. "You already met Gage, over there is Brass, Bronze, Ash, and Big Red."

So far these were definitely men and Bargavon quickly got the perception these were not their actual names but for lack of better understanding, the names they were referred to or perceived as. The remainder of the squad looked less than human, and they were a strange lot. Big Blue continued with introductions; there was Smiling Gold, who was the individual that was working on Bargavon's wounds during his retrieval from the desert. Big Blue called him a battle medic, but then looked at Baragvon and changed the wording to healer.

Next was Corona. The humanoid was tall and deep black. He reminded Bargavon of his dark warrior aspect but around him was a halo of silvery blue light tinged with purple. His frame was solidly built, and the blackness was continuous with whatever equipment, armor or weaponry he had. Bargavon could perceive or feel that the individual was smiling despite not seeing any delineating features of such.

"Welcome human," said Corona with a deep voice that seemed to echo through the massive black frame as if emanating from his entire structure. As Baragvon shook his massive hand, it seemed as if he were almost pulled into pulled into a sky of translucent glowing blackness with clouds of glowing amber and dark gold. The sudden sensation made Bargavon gasp unexpectedly. Corona let go the grasp and chuckled for a moment.

"That's Chant," said Big Blue pointed to a massive Baboon looking humanoid that was pulling on a hauberk of thick metal links similar to his own chainmail. The metal was strange in that it was a shimmering blue-black. It looked over at Bargavon, nodded and then went back to checking its gear, all the while humming and chanting an eerie melody that seemed too hauntingly beautiful to come from such a monstrous face. His exposed massive arms and down his legs had glowing silvery hued striped markings or tattoo's that softly rippled in time with the humming.

"And finally, Cobra. Like you, she's a bit of an anomaly. We kind of picked her up along the way on one of runs. Never had one of her kind actually want to join us."

Bargavon looked upon this warrior. He could tell she was a female by the beautiful almost human-like face and the noticeable curves of her breasts and hips. She stood a bit taller than Bargavon at around six feet and her build was strong and athletic. Her skin was of dull reddish black and when she approached, Bargavon realized that what he thought was fine mesh armor was her scaled skin. Her hair was long and black and pulled back in a ponytail. Upon her head protruded 2 small black horns and what he originally thought were strange footwear actually were cloven hooves. A lion-like tail draped down from her tailbone and swished about lazily. Despite all this she exuded powerful sexuality and Bargavon could feel himself almost pull toward her. She seemed to notice his interest and met his gaze. Her large almond shaped eyes were a bright yellow with a black snake-like pupil and their gaze reminded Bargavon instantly of the Snake God.

"She's a ..."

"Devil," interrupted Big Blue. "Yep, we picked her up on a run into one of the Hells. Can't remember which one though, after a while they all start to blend together. "I guess she got tired of tormenting your kind and sought something better."

Cobra smiled at Bargavon. He wasn't sure if it was a friendly smile or predatory.

A sound broke over the company of men preparing for the mission. To Bargavon it had both an auditory component as well as a visceral sensation through his body like a vibration. It was words, but it also had the quality of a volcano erupting far away and great waves crashing on the shore. It was restrained, as if to keep one safe from being blown apart. It came from the biggest warrior in the ship. He was massive and appeared to stand over ten feet tall. His form seemed human like except in size. He was clad in heavy interlocking plates of golden metal. Across his back a great scabbard held a sword six feet in length. He wore a golden helm. His face was mostly concealed by a metal mouth and jaw guard that allowed only his eyes and upper part of his face to be seen. His skin seemed of deep blue-black and it shimmered slightly with what looked like pinpoint glowing sparks of light slowly moving as if within him. Almost like someone had bent a dark star filled sky and formed it into a face. His eyes had no pupils, only the solid blue like the deepest blue of a glacial lake.

"All squad leaders check in with me. Drop zone is Outer River, Gorge Bravo. Assign retrieval teams."

Big Blue turned to Bargavon. "That's the Commander. I'll be right back. Gage, he's with you on this. You'll have him on a retrieval team today. We might as well have him dive right in." Big Blue turned and shouldered his massive bulk through the crowd of warriors toward the Commander.

Bargavon looked to Gage, he picked up that they were going into a combat zone but what were they retrieving? Gage sat him down on a bench and dropped down with a heavy thud next to him.

"Listen, here's the short of it. All of us here," he indicated to everyone in the ship's hold, "We all have done some bad shit. We were soldiers, mercenaries, killers, assassins, and murderers. You name it, if it involved a lot of violence and you're good at it then it's kind of a like a required certification to get you in the company. After we died or were killed back in the Dense as we like to call it here, you know, the physical world, we had to make amends for all the bad shit we did. You know like karmic debt and that bullshit."

Bargavon nodded, his grasp on Karma was still at a neophyte's understanding. Most of the Medregorian pantheon of gods sent you to some sort of afterlife where you dwelt in the halls of that particular god's kingdom for eternity unless you were evil and you were sent to one of the Ninety-nine Hells. Gage saw that Bargavon was having some trouble with the concept and gave him a quick lesson on Karma. That it was a universal law no matter where you came from in the Universe.

Suddenly there was an unusual drop in the hull, like the ship hit a deep swell, then another, longer drop, then another, dropping, dropping. Bargavon felt his stomach dropping right along with it. It was like the bottom of the sea kept dropping out. He had rode through some bad stormy seas before but the swells outside must be enormous.

Gage broke off from his discussion on karma and spiritual debt. He grabbed onto some equipment webbing behind him due to the rolling and rocking of the hull. "It's like this when we go deeper. Gotta push through those containment walls. Feels like waves don't it?" He cracked a smile at Bargavon. Bargavon hoped his white-knuckled grip on the bench wasn't being noticed and smiled back with gritted teeth.

Gage appeared to be quite relaxed and his body rocked with the ship as he continued, "Anyway, back to what I was saying. We're all here paying off our debt. We could either rot in some sort of hell or crawl into some lonely dark crevasse in the universe feeling terrible about our actions, cry about it, and suck our thumbs and spend a few millennia in torment or…" Gage waved his hands around and then slapped his palms against his metal breastplate, "this!"

Bargavon raised his eyebrows, "Battle? We fight off our karmic debt by going to battle every day in the afterlife like the Northman stories?"

"Erm, sort of." Gage scratched his chin stubble. "More like we go into the dark places of the Universe and extract lost souls and return them to the Aperture so they can proceed on with their evolution."

"I am aware of many religions in my world talk about angelic beings doing such jobs."

Gage laughed. "That's a fucking laugh. Leave it to any religion of any race to twist a fucking truth." Gage reached into a metal box and started putting what looked like small cylindrical quarrel points into his metallic black crossbow through a small covered port in the side of it. He continued without looking up. "Those angels or whatever they are vibrate too brightly, too fast. The lost souls deep down can't see them. Aren't aware of them and so can't be rescued or helped. That's where we come in. We're kind of like the dog soldiers, the grunts. Listen man, to a living person in the Dense, we're like ghosts. To put it one way, our frequency is faster than the those in the Dense but you wouldn't confuse us in the 'Ascended Beings' category. We vibe closer to the lost souls, they can see us and we can pull them out and get them to the Aperture where we hand them off to the so-called angels or loved ones from beyond or whatever."

"What do you mean 'whatever'? Don't you know?"

"Naw, not really. I saw some real bright lights a couple times when we had to do some extractions in the upper zones. That might have been them."

Gage looked over Bargavon for a moment. "Chainmail, sword and ax. You like to work in close. They'll be plenty of that in a few minutes. You want to take the helmet too? It's yours." Bargavon looked behind him and found a helmet with a mail neck guard exactly like his back in the physical hanging on a rack. He reached for it and strapped it on.

"Ok, a few things. One, if it isn't a company warrior, kill it, and yes things can die here, well, sort of. Let's just say their essence that forms a body here is dispersed and scattered for a while and its back to square one or two or three, hell I don't know. That knowledge is way above my paygrade. Two, you're on a retrieval team today with me and Bronze. Look for a mark, a soul that is ready for retrieval. You will know because they will make eye contact with you, literally reach out to you. You grab them and help them or carry them if you have to back to the ship. The rest of the squad will cover you. Three, we leave no one behind. Got it?"

Before Bargavon could reply the hull slammed hard into something violently jarring the ship to a halt. The warrior named Bronze who had worked his way near Gage and Bargavon turned to them, "It's like they don't even try a soft landing."

A large door opened up on the side of the hull. Warriors of the company raced out the door in close order, weapons drawn. Packed in formation, out they poured down the ramp to a rocky plateau. A sight greeted Bargavon that would make most mortal men go mad. It was a scene from the one of the religious scriptures of the Ninety-nine hells. A vast land of smoking mountains, lakes of lava, pits of roiling smoke and noxious gas. The sky was impossibly black and the light of the place seem to be cast only from the fire itself rising from innumerable pits and crevasses. The sound of millions of tortured souls rent the air along with roars of beasts and the sound of great crunching noises of teeth on bone and bleating sounds.

The company fanned out in an arc and readied their weapons in anticipation. Within a few heartbeats there was an explosion of violence and combat. Their swords, spears, axes and other strange weapons rose and fell in great arcs sweeping away scores of ghastly grey or charcoal colored bodies that seem to swarm up onto the plateau next to the side of the great ship. At first, he thought these were men but then he saw their features. Visages of goats, pigs, rams, lizards, snakes, vultures, apes and other detestable things beyond description.

Some had scaly bodies others had hard carapaces or bristly tufts of fur. They wielded clubs made of bones, or sharpened pieces of iron or just their own natural weaponry of tusk, talon, tooth and claw. Bargavon hesitated in awe for a couple seconds, trying to wrap his mind around the whole thing but couldn't. He did however understand battle and his training launched him into the fight in the next heartbeat. With his ax and longsword out, he plunged into the fray finding a space between Big Blue and Gage. These humanoid beasts although viscous and horrible to behold still recoiled back as his blades slashed and sunk into scale and hide, torso and limb. All were slashed and splintered by his blows and out spurted a black oily ichor from the grievous wounds he rent upon them. There were many more of these devilish beasts than there were of the company, whose numbers Bargavon guessed at perhaps a hundred.

Bone club, tusk and claw tore at his mail hauberk or upon his forearm or greave armored leg. They were strong and soon he was bleeding from several cuts. To either side his new-found comrades were laying waste about them with large heavy weapons cutting the vile beast-men in half or sending chunks of tattered black flesh flying through the noxious air. It was apparent this company of warriors was indeed both fearsome and effective. Within minutes scores of these devil bodies lay in ripped heaps upon the ground, black ichor formed growing pools about them and then a pause as there were no immediate enemies about them. The large golden hued commander ordered the company to advance into a deep cleft in the rock nearby.

"Head for the cleft and stay upon the trail. They will be just below it in the gorge," ordered the golden-hued commander. His armor splotched with the gore of his kills and his massive silvery sword looked as if coated in tar, a chunk of ichor-matted hide slid off it and onto the ground.

Big Blue looked down at Bargavon. "The fun part is over I think. You did well for your first time. Had a feeling you had the right skill sets. Now for the hard part, the retrieval, just stay with Gage and Bronze. They will show you how." Big Blue continued to the cleft following the Commander, he and the rest of the squad fell in with the other squads of the company. One squad remained on guard at the ramp into the ship.

The company marched down to the cleft in the sheer rock wall of a mountainside, and down into what was referred to as Gorge Bravo. The path was a zig-zagging course into a defile and soon the right side dropped away into a dark abyss. Something down there was roaring with a voice so deep it didn't even register as sound, only a sickening vibratory wave. It seemed some time before the defile opened a bit wider. The path remained about five feet wide and hugged a sheer rock wall, while the right dropped down into a river below. A river of mottled gray slowly moving past, but as the path descended lower to the river, shapes could be made out in the river, and then the overwhelming horror hit Bargavon.

This was not a river of muddy water but a river of bodies tumbling and roiling. Whether they were naked or in tattered clothing, all were a mottled color of grey as if they were dipped in clay and ash. Almost all wore a dead lifeless expression or a frozen face of terror, but no sound issued from them. The retrieval teams of the company spread out along the path near the river's edge. They were like fishermen ready to cast line and net. Their heads sweeping back and forth as the river of bodies rolled past. Bargavon could easily kneel down and grab one of them. A young woman caught his eye, beautiful of body, but ghastly in expression. He went to grasp her, but Bronze grasped his shoulder.

"No! Don't waste your time. She'll fade out by the time you get her to the ship. Look for those who are calling out or that make eye contact with you. Those we can save now. They are aware of us."

Bargavon returned his gaze back to the river and noted that some people were now aware of the soldiers lined upon the path just above them. At first a couple, then several and finally a score of voices called out. They cried out for help, they called on angels and deities, their gods, their loved ones. Some few pointed to the soldiers and cried out, "The angels have come. I am here, save me!"

Angels? Thought Bargavon, this company looked a far cry from angelic beings. They were armored men, or at least humanoid, many far bigger than him, some literal giants covered in black ichor upon their armor and they were a terrible and grim to behold. Bronze scooped up a man easily from the river who had called out to him. Gage grabbed another. Big Blue and the rest of the squad had fanned out, weapons drawn and remained on the lookout for enemies.

Soon a wretched looking woman called out to him. Bargavon looked to Gage, who was helping his own retrieval to his feet. Gage nodded affirmatively and so Bargavon reached down and pulled the woman up from the roiling mass. She was small and light and seemed exhausted, but grateful. He carried her in his arms away from the river. She repeatedly thanked her 'angel.'

"Now what?" he said as he looked about. Perhaps sixty people had been pulled from the human river. In his arms the woman looked up at him, tears filling her eyes, her arms clasped behind his neck as she continued to call him her angel.

Bargavon met her gaze. He was wooden in his response. He had no training in this. "I...have come.....for you...but I'm no angel."

"Hey, New Guy. If you were in this place for an eon and got pulled out by someone. You'd be calling them an angel too," chided Gage supporting the rescued man as they walked back toward the path.

The commander bellowed "Form up and move out! Vanguard and Rearguard ranks form up!" Those not holding onto or carrying a person drew forth weapons and either took a forward or rear guard position while the rest were kept to the protected center.

Big Blue and the others started to fall in around the line of retrieval teams and those that they retrieved. The armored Rhino like humanoid lumbered next to Bargavon. "To these poor wretches waking up from a long duration of suffering, we glow like angelic beings, as hard as it is to believe," chuckled Big Blue. "So I'm told."

The woman wept softly on his shoulder as Bargavon still was trying to process everything. Killing was easy. Two decades of experience and relentless training made it as natural as eating and sleeping. Compassion, empathy and kindness, those feelings were in a space he had not walked in very often for many years. *Long time, not since...*

Bargavon's thought was interrupted by Big Blue next to him "Told you this was the harder part. You got to relearn that whole empathy and compassion thing again."

"They kind of beat it out of me in training," said Bargavon thinking back to the brutal methods used to break down the young conscripts and then rebuild them in the image the Imperial army and navy wanted.

"Gage, you're a goddamn human. Help this new guy figure out his sappy, confusing, convoluted emotions will yah? My race just keeps it all pretty simple and straightforward," said Big Blue.

"Sure, Sarge," said Gage guiding his man up the cinder like path. He turned to Bargavon. "You got to feel your way through it. You learn as you go. This is how we unload the debt. We got to help people, help those in need. We get these lost souls back to the ship and back to the Aperture. We would give our life to protect each and every one of them in the process. That is the way through our servitude to work off all the misery we have delivered onto others." Gage finished and looked down at the woman Bargavon was carrying. "Act as if she was your girlfriend, your sister or your mother."

Bargavon was silent the rest of the way back out of the Gorge. He could hear occasional fighting at the front or back of the line but it seemed the vanguard and rear guard units kept the devil spawn away from the Retrieval Teams.

The company moved up the defile and soon left what was known as Bravo Gorge. They arrived back at the plateau, but the ship was gone, only the heaps of dead devils remained. The commander drew forth a great horn and a peal of sound pierced the heavy drab air. A moment later, a thundering cascading pillar of light plummeted out of the black sky and there before them a massive troop transport ship materialized and a large portal opened in the hull. The ramp was lowered and the warriors entered leading the rescued people within. These people sat or stood alongside their rescuers, some were overcome with emotion, but most seemed a bit in shock. The woman that Bargavon had retrieved from the human river was in a deep sleep in his arms, wet tears had partially cleaned away the mask of ash and slag from her cheeks.

A massive individual nearly the height of the commander lumbered past the squad as they were settling in. The thing seemed to be a humanoid edifice of petrified rock or at least resembled it. It was covered in black ichor nearly head to toe. As he passed, Big Blue reached out and grabbed him with a massive hand.

"Did it get a little hairy when we left for the gorge?"

"Yeah. The reserve squad nearly got overrun. They're working on Smoke now. He got it bad. We had to pull out of the sector and wait until you called us back."

Blue patted him on the shoulder and sat down to work the intricate layer of metal plating off his jaw and snout. Armor anatomically fitted to the rhino being.

There was a return of the rocking of the hull that signaled to Bargavon that the ship was again moving. He was not sure how long the gentle floating rocking lasted as time seemed to be a malleable element here. The movement in the hull finally ended and the massive door dropped open. The woman he had retrieved was roused and she looked about in a daze.

Big Blue turned to Bargavon and pointed to the door. "Lead her out to the Aperture. You cannot miss it. Just guide her and let her go. That's all you need to do now."

Outside was simply what can only be described as an aperture. A brilliant horizontal line of white light, a light so bright the surrounding environment seemed like darkness but Bargavon was not so sure that was the case. The rescued people were led off the ramp and toward the light. The woman

Bargavon rescued was able to walk and as she neared the Aperture, her pace quickened. She let go of his hand and started to jump and run. He heard laughter from her as she ran. Movement was seen coming from the light, but Bargavon could not make out details. Soon the other rescued people started calling out names, perhaps loved ones, family, spouses, or friends. They had recognition of these people within the light. Others started running to the light and disappeared within its brightness. When the last one disappeared the warriors from the retrieval teams stood there solemnly for a moment. Each filled with a sudden longing to enter the Aperture and what lay beyond. They could not, even if they tried for it was closed to them. The temporal concept of 'someday' lingered on their thoughts for a few moments. They had a job to do, a dirty, dangerous job that only they could do, for they were the angels' dark helpers. They slowly turned one by one and filed back into the hull of the waiting ship suspended there in the endless darkness.

The return to the physical world or to the Dense as Gage referred to it provided him an almost serene existence in contrast to his nightly journeys. During the day he managed his men stationed in the city of Sawarbad. No combat action was taking place at the time. Mundane drilling and patrols were the norm.

At night, however, he found himself immediately in the cargo hold of the transport ship as the company headed off on another run. Often times this was in some dreary or dark place retrieving the lost souls wherever they may be and where angels could not tread. Sometimes violent combat was required against dark beings bent on ripping the life out of the warriors but always being defeated by what Bargavon perceived as some of the strongest, most skilled and violent team of warriors he had ever served with. These men or beings in some cases in the company were terrible to behold. All could match the violence or brutality being thrown against them. In some cases many were literally plucked near the gates of Hell themselves.

Bargavon stayed in Big Blue's squad and was on the retrieval team about half the time. Each foray brought him better proficiency at handling his retrieval. His awkwardness began to soften a little, but it was work. He enjoyed being on the attack and guard teams where his honed skills of combat fed his natural high.

Bargavon learned there were many dark places in the vastness of the Universe besides the many versions of Hell. There were dead lost voids, lonely dark pits removed of all light, self- created constructs of malice, torment or suffering that required the company to fight or break through. There were even forces and beings that simply delighted in feeding off the negative energy these souls emitted. These were dealt with as well. Sometimes through threat of violence or at other times direct violence which was a specialty of the Company.

Chapter 6

Consequences of Actions

After a month in Sawarbad, the Medregorian army returned to Kathvitora and for Bargavon to the warm embrace of Krin and the company of his father. For Krin, he brought back a coffer of exotic perfumes, scented oils, and golden bangles he purchased in the bustling markets. For Rhiavar, a local Jassurian noble in gave him a set of Yendessi playing pieces carved from rare blue and purple hued tanzanite stone.

Rhiavar immediately cleared the Yendessi boards and set up the shiny new pieces. Father and son got down to their game, Bargavon going over every detail of the battle and described the colorful markets of Sawarbad, the bright white-washed buildings and the narrow winding cobblestone streets that often tumbled into out of the way courts that may have a hidden tavern or a shop selling hard to find artifacts or an opium den. His father relayed rumors of trouble with the city-state of Wuxano to the East and that military action might be initiated. At least, that is what Bargavon's officer friends told Rhiavar during their Yendessi beat down sessions with him while he was away in Sawarbad.

Bargavon's nightly retrievals began to have an effect upon his demeanor. Subtlety at first, but then even Krin started to notice. He became calmer and kinder, especially with her. He held her longer, sometimes he brought her the wine, or asked her to accompany him on errands throughout the city which he had seldom done before. His mood had always been grim by default, lost in thought working out a stratagem or going over military procedures or schedules. He was serious about his command and often it carried over into his off hours. He began to show more genuine humanness outside of intimate encounters with Krin and Yendessi conversations with his father. Having a broader vision of reality made him appreciate the time with Krin and his father.

Krin awoke one morning. Bargavon had been up for a while by the looks of him. He was fully dressed and was drinking tea from a cup. He had placed another next to her side of the bed. It's aroma of orange peel and ginger aroused her from her sleep as Bargavon had snuck back in quiet as a fox. He stood there leaning against the doorframe that led out to the bedroom balcony. The cool morning air gently drifted in and the sun had risen over the rooftops of the nearby buildings spilling its warm light onto the balcony and across the tiled floor up to the bedsheets coloring the white linen in a warm golden hue. The sun was behind the muscular frame of her master creating a silhouette effect and a halo-like aura of golden light.

"You look like an angel, Bargavon. But I know that cannot be true for you're a devil." She smiled reaching for the steaming cup of tea. She took a sip and then pondered a moment, "No, I am wrong, only an angel would bring me tea. Thank you, Master," she said smiling sweetly.

There was something in his demeanor at her statement that made him flinch. It was subtle, but she could read him quite well and he stood there silently, his eyes never breaking contact with hers. A long silent moment went by, Krin frowned a bit. Baragvon seemed to be acting rather strangely. Usually by now he would be pressed upon her. He was almost always aroused in the morning. Krin did not mind at all for she matched him in her sexual needs. She came from a people that enjoyed it and Bargavon was sexually generous partner satisfying her needs as well. She set her tea on the table and slowly pulled away the sheets revealing her flawless northern fair skin, her taut body and sensuous curves that could drag a man's eyes across it magnetically.

"I now find an ugliness upon you that I cannot bear anymore," stated Bargavon flatly.

Krin's voice caught in her throat. She stammered but couldn't get out a reply so sudden, unexpected and hurtful his words were. Emotion began to well up in her for she truly loved him despite the imperial custom of her being his slave. He had treated her so well all this time. He had never hurt her or treated her poorly, nor had any harsh or hurtful words until now.

He slowly stepped toward the bed. Krin was still too much in shock to pull the covers up over her nakedness. His face took on the stern grimness she had seen thousands of times before but never directed at her.

"I meant this," he said bitterly grabbing her ankle and eyeing the slave anklet. He drew forth the key from his pocket and unlocked the adornment that proclaimed to every citizen in the Empire that she was someone's property. He pulled it off her and flung it across the room where it clattered across the tiles. He gently placed her leg back upon the bed and looked deep into her eyes. Tears that were started as hurt, transformed into a mixture of emotions that poured from her as she embraced the man she once called master and wept cradled against his neck.

Bargavon held her close. What was occurring beyond the Veil was reverberating back into the world of the Dense. There was no going back to what he once was. He was changing inside and for the first time since he was conscripted into the military he felt uncertainty of his actions, his path, his life here in the physical world. Most of all, he had just freed Krin and secretly feared she would leave him. He realized he loved her and it made him feel vulnerable. It was a feeling he had not afforded himself as a warrior and officer of the Medregorian Empire, until now.

That night Bargavon was moving through a desolate landscape with Big Blue's Squad. It was a place where the Company swept from time to time. Occasional lost souls would stray here and never find their way out. They arrived and fanned out seeking any cries for help or other such signals of despair or loss. Brass and Ash each found someone and after a time Big Blue called for the Squad to return back to the ship and rendezvous with the other units.

Suddenly, Bargavon felt something pass by his legs and disappear into the gloom. He felt no alarm nor any menace. A small presence then emerged out of the bleak landscape in front of him. It was in the shape of a dog. He focused and yes, it was a dog, and a very particular dog at that. It was the one he tried to save after the battle of Ahrza. Its body was slightly aglow as if it radiated light from within it and it seemed to have a spectral quality to it. The light was soft, pale yellow and seemed to emit a feeling of friendship, loyalty and happiness from it.

"It's a dog that I tried to save after a battle. What is it doing out here?" said Bargavon quite perplexed.

"Sometimes animals and other intelligent life forms are attracted to us out here, that one must have bonded to you somehow," said Gage. The dog came up and started licking Bargavon's hand.

"Keep it, might come in handy. They have their senses enhanced on this side of the Veil as well." Gage reached down and petted it, the dog responded by wagging its tail.

Bargavon bent down and looked the dog in the face and stroked it as well. "Okay dog, if you wish to follow me stay out of the way. It is dangerous, ugly business we do. You are free to go at any time if you so wish. Welcome to the Company then."

Bronze was moving past Bargavon to change places with Chant in the lead position. He looked down and smiled at the dog, "Who do we have here?"

Bargavon looked down at the dog and back to Bronze, "I haven't given him a name. Should he have one?"

"Yeah, it will act as an Ident from which we can locate him, if we needed to."

Bargavon thought for a moment. "He shall be called Valor." The dog wagged his tail and seemed to brighten at the name.

"Why Valor? He doesn't look like an attack dog or guard dog?" said Bronze perplexed at such a strong name for such a scrappy looking dog.

"He stood alone between his master and several armed men and gave his life selflessly."

"He did! Then, he belongs with the Company. Welcome aboard Valor."

And so Valor, the dog, became an unofficial Company mascot. In future missions, they found him valuable in locating lost souls, warning of hidden danger that missed their surveillance and Valor would often sit with the retrievals to comfort them.

The Dark Warrior sat upon a rocky ledge overlooking a landscape of hues of grey. No color fell upon the scene, a muted grayness of barren hills and rocky steppe land. A dry ravine snaked below. The form of the strange tattooed brown man that just talked with him was working his way along it. He strode confidently among the rocks with his staff. The strange but wise individual had found him here and had told him much about his violent counterpart. His words were still settling into his consciousness. "You must get his attention. Show him. Make him see. You are the protector he created. He cannot progress until he faces what he fears."

He looked down at his hands. They were impenetrable ebony appendages that held no detail, only an outline filled in like ink. So this is what he was. The reality was none too comforting. Only vague memories not directly related to his purpose passed through his mind and seemed to break apart if his consciousness fell upon them. All he knew was his name was Bargavon, he was very good at fighting and his sole purpose was to protect the secret he carried within him; a heavy memory that he was to keep safe and pure.

He thought back to his earliest memory. There was a great ripping sound and he felt as if he had been torn from something. The next thing he remembered was the warrior who happened to look like him violently attacked him, as if to snuff out, to destroy the secret he so dearly protected. Bargavon put himself between the brightly glowing warrior and what he carried. Long they fought for they seemed almost equals. Bargavon knew little except the secret was precious to him and nothing in the dismal gloom of this place would take it from him.

Bargavon saw a set of bright eyes bobbing near the edge of light. He rose drawing forth ax and sword warily. The creature entered the light, it was a dog. He seemed friendly and wagged his tail and made his way over to him unafraid. Bargavon was curious for he had seen little here that seemed beneficent. He allowed the dog to stay. He wondered what it was like to have joy or happiness. It seemed when he searched his memory for these feelings all that came to him were sadness, grief, hate and rage. *Perhaps that is all that was given to me.*

Bargavon found himself moving again. There was no time here, only one unbroken moment. His black form glided through the textured black landscape that seemed only lightly rendered of substance and form. The dog had stayed for a time and then seemed to perk up as if it heard a call that only he could hear. It bolted away from the ledge and off into the darkness. Bargavon quickly strode after the dog. The journey ended at a dock where Bargavon could see strange warriors entering a massive war galley tied to a dock. Heading up the ramp was the violent bright warrior adversary that looked like him. He had to find a way to reveal the secret to his twin, a part of himself that could pass back into the Dense.

Chapter 7

Dream Temples & Not So Fond Memories

Bargavon stood before the Temple of Acroiyer, The God of Dreams. *Of course, I end up here. Where else would I have ended up, very peculiar indeed.* The edifice was much like many of the other temples, chapels and shrines along Temple Street. Each one had its street face decorated with stone columns, reliefs and carvings, statuary and other stonework all beautifully sculpted by the best artisans of Kathvitora. The street was a cacophony of bells, chimes, gongs, drumming and chanting all coming from one temple or another and sometimes several at once. So too were ones olfactory senses bombarded with a cascade of various incenses, flowers or even blood from a fresh slaughter of a sacrificial goat or calf. This was the street where all of Medregor's ninety-nine gods had their official houses of worship. Parishioners winded their way through the crowds mixed with pilgrims from far away as well as the colored robes and outfits of priests, monks and high clerics.

Bargavon tracked the man to this temple. He originally saw him on Lamp-maker Street. The man he followed here was tall by Medregorian standards at over six and half feet in height. He was bald with a grey white goatee and striking blue eyes. He was dressed in some simple brown robes, the front of which were splotched with colored pigments, as if he had wiped his hands on them for his hands were stained with many colors. Bargavon had first caught sight of him leaving a shop that ground colored pigments for dyes or paints.

This man he had followed to the temple intrigued Bargavon for he recognized this individual from beyond the Veil. He was or at least greatly resembled the robed man with the slate and writing implements seen near the fringes of a couple of the Company's runs. *Could this man travel beyond the Veil as well?* He had to find out.

Once inside the dark and cool interior, Bargavon closed the thick door. The sounds and smells of the street were shut out completely. Inside was an ante chamber decorated with intricate carved stone and inset with semi-precious stones such as white scolecite, green hued malachite and purple amethysts. Curtains of soft purple opened to a main hall with a high domed ceiling painted with a full moon in a deep blue sky speckled with stars. Sidewall paintings showed dreamy pastoral scenes, ocean scenes with the waves reflecting the starry sky above, and woodland scenes all under soft moonlight. The chamber was set with soft couches, cushioned mats and pillows. A few large candles placed in silvered mirror lanterns gave a soft glow to the chamber. The glass panes of the lanterns were stained with soft cool colors of blue, purple and green. The sound of soft wooden flute or chimes would occasionally float in from another chamber nearby. There was an incense burner giving off a pleasant dreamy fragrance.

"We encourage states of dreaming here at the Temple. We lead our worshippers into dream states to explore beyond. That is our method of worship here," spoke a calm voice from the doorway leading to another part of the temple. The man was dressed in robes of cerulean blue trimmed with soft purple and gold. He was middle-aged with black hair streaked with grey. He had handsome features and a permanent smile upon his lips. He introduced himself as Thossa, High Priest of Acroiyer, The God of Dreams.

Bargavon started to introduce himself but Thossa held up a hand, "I know who you are. Captain Bargavon, Warrior, Hero of Medregor, King-slayer of Tondra Pass, shall I go on?" smiled Thossa. "You are easy to recognize in Kathvitora Captain. I am curious as to why a man of your profession has come to the Temple of Acroiyer. Very unusual. If your type worship at all, it's usually down by the temples of Tarques, Achimir or perhaps Juum for safe journeys across the sea or even Kasemus for luck.

"I followed a tall man in brown paint stained robes from Lampmaker Street to this temple. I need to speak with him."

Thossa looked somewhat concerned, "Yes, that would be Falsk. He just returned from getting more materials for painting. He is a resident monk and the artist whose work you see about you," said Thossa pointing to the painting upon the walls and ceiling. "Is there some sort of trouble?"

"No trouble, I just need some questions answered. May I have a few words with him?"

"Certainly, come this way Captain." Thossa lead Bargavon down a hallway past several smaller chambers and down a winding set of stone steps to a lower level where they came upon a workroom. There in the chamber was the man Bargavon had followed mixing gold powder into a paint base. Somehow in the few short minutes he was here, he had already gotten flecks of it on his beard and forehead.

"Bargavon, this is Falsk, one of the temple monks and our resident artist and scribe. Brother Falsk, I present to you Captain Bargavon."

"Captain, it is an honor to have such a hero of the Empire here for a visit," said Falsk bending into a bow, the stirring rod used to mix the paint swept a gold streak across the front of robe. Bargavon keenly observed that the monk did indeed recognize him, but more importantly he got the feeling his arrival here was not unexpected.

Bargavon gave a polite greeting in return and began to wander about the chamber looking at the works in progress. There was work tables upon which sat ceramic or stone carvings or molds. A large wooden panel stood in the corner half painted of people floating on clouds under a smiling moon. On a cluttered table was a large tome with vellum sheets being illuminated with gold leaf paint and colored ink. Between and among these areas were all the tools of the trade and materials for sculpting, painting and scribing. The works in progress were obviously works of a master.

"Tell me Brother Falsk, where do you get the inspiration to create such works."

Falsk smiled and said "Captain, in my dreams I travel to other realms beyond the gross denseness of this world. My creativity and design are brought forth from those realms beyond and simply made manifest by my hands."

"Ever travel to the Ninety-nine Hells?"

A knowing smile spread across the monk's face. "As an artist I paint and mold not only the beatific, but also the horrific should the qualities of such be required for a project."

Bargavon stopped and looked down at a painting that was more than half finished but even in that state was a beautiful work of art. "Like this one?"

He was staring upon the painted description of his company beyond the Veil pulling humans in distress from a raging river. Near the river's edge were devilish creatures torturing and terrorizing the humans. Some of the company soldiers had gone down to fight with them as other soldiers were aiding those in the river. The soldiers wore splendid Medregorian armor and weaponry and looked most handsome and noble. Above them in the sky were angelic beings of light in white and golden flowing robes with wings painted of brilliant white and highlighted with gold. They seemed to be pointing and directing the Medregorian soldiers. Beyond the angels in the dark and dreary sky were golden stairs leading up to a silvery cloud.

"And which one is me?" said Bargavon getting closer to the painting and inspecting the faces carefully

Falsk did not seem surprised at Bargavon's question. He walked over to the painting and bent to examine it. He looked carefully at Bargavon and back to the painting. "This is you pulling out the woman," hovering a brush over the surface.

"Curious though, all the soldiers look to be Medregorian warriors and we both know that is not the case. Nor do I remember the angels present," stated Bargavon, raising his brow

"I have taken some artistic liberties of course as people viewing the work must be able to grasp the concept of it."

"So, obviously, I am not the first man you have met here in the Dense that you have actually seen beyond the Veil."

115

Falsk stood up from the painting. "No Captain, you are not. A small handful only, but you are the first I have met that is involved in such a noble act of retrieving lost souls."

"My choice in that was rather limited. I do not think noble quite captures the experience," He replied looking again down at the beautiful painting.

Bargavon was impressed and curious. He had many questions and was fortunate that Thossa and Falsk were willing to talk at length with him about their experiences. Over the next few weeks Bargavon gained insight and knowledge with their talks into the nature of reality beyond the Veil, its inhabitants and some of the locales the dream priests were familiar with. They were aware only academically of the Jaguar God and the pantheon of the gods worshipped by the jungle people.

Of the Dark Warrior, they postulated that he was an unresolved fragmented aspect of Bargavon and that it was protecting or shielding some sort of hurt or wound from earlier in his life. The split of this Dark Warrior occurred during the Shamanic mystical rite that Bargavon had unwittingly initiated. Although the dream priests of Acroiyer were not familiar with the Shamanic customs or rituals, they assumed some sort of break down and then reintegration of one's soul was part of the Shamanic rite of passage. Being that Bargavon was unprepared for the ritual prevented the rift of his soul from being properly reintegrated. Their counsel was for Bargavon to find the Shaman again and to somehow find a way to uncover the hidden wound and reclaim the aspect of the Dark Warrior back into him. That was the problem. He carried with him the stone totem about his neck of the Jaguar God, both in the Dense and beyond the Veil, but as Mokantai had told him in the jungle, it was for the Shaman to find him, not the other way around.

On one of his visits to the Temple of Acroiyer, Bargavon was hailed by a largish man at a cross street just outside the Temple District. He stopped as the man smiled and jogged across the busy cobblestone street with a noticeable limp to his gait. When he got close Bargavon recognized him, his name was Vasardev from Cordoba. He served in one of Bargavon special heavy squads. He was honorably relieved of active duty due to a severe leg wound at the battle of Ahrza. Bargavon clasped his hands warmly.

"How are you Vasardev. Barring the limp you look quite well man."

"I am, Sir. The leg is as good as it is going to get unfortunately," replied Vasardev

"What can I do for you?"

"Sir, I am discharged from the army, but I was wondering if you knew of any positions I could still be suited for. I am not really suited for mercantile or labor if you catch my meaning."

Bargavon thought for a moment. "I'll check with the citadel and garrison. They should be able to find something for you, especially with my recommendation. You served me well Vasardev. I promise to look into it. A man of your bearing can't be selling apples from a cart the rest of his life." And so Bargavon was able to get Vasardev employed as a jailor in the palace dungeons. The pay was fair and suited the large man's previous skill sets. This chance meeting and simple act would later have far reaching implications upon Bargavon's life.

During this time Bargavon found Krin to be a wellspring of happiness and joy in his life. Despite freeing her, she remained with him willingly. When not on official military duties, he spent time with her around the beautiful sites around Kathvitora. He allowed himself the enjoyment of a proper courtship of a woman engaging in the activities that he could not when she was a slave. It was the happiest time of his adult life for the very few months that it lasted.

Nightly his routine still consisted of retrievals with the company and occasional wanderings in the dark looking for his dark warrior. Two events beyond the Veil were quite significant during this time. The first occurred aboard the transport after a retrieval run one night.

The sound of Big Red's laughter in the last battle gnawed at Bargavon. He had heard it before and it was the laughter during the battle that brought out what may be a very strange coincidence. Back on the transport Bargavon looked across at Big Red. He was a large Northman, his hair and beard long and golden-red, his frame massive with thick cords of muscle and sinew was draped in his golden mail hauberk and he wielded a heavy ax two handed in battle. Bargavon's eyes fell upon his wide leather belt that hung a dagger scabbard which held the standard wide double bladed heavy Northman dagger. It was a weapon that he had never seen drawn before. Big Red had caught his gaze and Bargavon saw a fierce glint of secret knowing.

Big Red's white teeth shown through his beard "You interested in my dagger Medregorian? Here have a look then."

Big Red drew it forth and handed it across the walkway, pommel first. Bargavon reached out and took it. The weight felt exactly as he thought it would, the pommel was familiar and the blade, edged on both sides with the familiar sawtooth section. It was, however, the engraved raven and wolf on either side of the blade that tied everything together. This was the very dagger he took off the dead Northman king at the Tondra Pass years ago, a battle that made Bargavon a hero and accelerated his rise through the ranks.

Despite the cold chill that ran up his spine, Bargavon remained outwardly impassive. "It's a fine blade, well balanced and well crafted," handing the blade back across the walkway.

"Like the one you carry as well?" said Big Red, his eyes resting on Bargavon's own dagger scabbard. Bargavon did not answer. His was identical to Big Red's. Not the same type or make. It was the very same dagger.

Big Red took the blade and leaned forward to lock eyes with Bargavon. "This is the blade you have back across the Veil. You took it from me after you removed my head with my own ax." For a moment their eyes were locked, and that battle was relived in full in a matter of seconds, the dagger held between both their hands bridged the memory from another time and another denser reality.

Bargavon thought back to that day up in the Tondra Pass along the Northern Marches. It was late Fall and the battle took place in the blowing snow of that cold pass. The Northern Barbarians were using the pass to launch a last grand raid into the border towns before the winter snows blocked the passes. Scouts reported a force a couple thousand strong heading south. Bargavon was a sergeant at that time and in charge of a squad of heavy footmen. They were stationed at a garrison town along the border near Tondra Pass. They were part of the company under Captan Cythruul who was one of several captains of the army stationed there.

The Imperial army assembled and moved up into the pass to repel the invaders. The next day found both forces in battle against each other. Both sides expected the other to be there and the battle turned into a stand-up slug fest. For the first few hours neither side could claim they were winning but both sides could claim a lot of dead. For Bargavon, the battle was grueling and not only because the Northmen were such strong adversaries but also because of the snowstorm that decided to break during the battle. The men were in cold weather gear, but wind and snow never are helpful to running an organized battle. Eventually the battle lines broke down to isolated pockets of men fighting in the cold wind-blown pass.

Bargavon's squad was near a high point upon a rocky mound. At the beginning of the battle it commanded a good view of the pass and was of strategic importance. It was a narrowed area that once taken, would allow the Northman to fan outward and punch through the stretched defensive formations of the Medregorians. Captain Cythruul kept his company here for that very reason.

The Northmen knew this as well and they committed many warriors to take it. This became the turning point of the battle. Over the hour the Medregorians were being driven backward up to the top of the rocky mound and the fight came to Bargavon's squad that was held back in reserve for reinforcing the crumbling line. Cythruul gave the order and Sergeant Bargavon's and two squads committed to the battle line.

The Northmen were larger than their southern Medregorian neighbors and were strong and stupidly fearless. Their armor was variable, but they wielded well-made axes, spears and longswords. The Medregorians were better armored with mail, helmets and shields. The Imperial army fought in well-ordered lines or one of several standard formations that they drilled in maximizing their effectiveness as an integrated fighting unit. They also relied on missile troops such as archers and javelin armed skirmishers to soften up their enemy. The howling wind and blowing snow did not allow them this advantage today. The Northmen fought very well that day and smashed through the lines in a few places rushing up to claim the peak and tear down the Imperial standard. The Medregorians were beginning to fold.

It was at this point Captain Cythruul took a battle ax to the head quickly ending his tenure as company commander and a living human being. Sensing a collapse in morale, Bargavon quickly ordered his men into a counterattack, he led the charge toward where the captain had fallen. The captain was slain by an armored giant of a Northman. Six foot seven inches of sinew and bone under a hauberk of mail that went down to his knees. His full helm gilded with gold indicated he may be a jarl or king.

As Bargavon plunged through the snow, he saw this Northman lord clear two more Medregorians from in front of him with a sweep of his battle ax, one of whom was the Medregorian standard bearer. The men about him were well armed and armored as well. Under fur cloaks and boots were chainmail hauberks, or steel ringmail. Their weapons were longswords, hand and battle axes as well as spears. Most had steel helmets and wooden round shields with iron bosses. The ground around them was littered with the dead and the dying, broken weapons, shattered shields, and spreading pools of blood standing out starkly against the accumulating field of white snow.

Bargavon raced toward their leader. Behind him were seasoned Medregorian soldiers quite experienced in fighting these Northmen raiders. On the way to his man, Bargavon fetched up a javelin stuck in a dead body and hurled it at the giant. The wind carried it to the left and the Northman didn't even move, laughing at the perceived poor throw. His laughing continued even as Bargavon crossed his sword with the Northman's ax. The battle was on. The Medregorians and Northmen came together in a collision of metal on metal and metal on flesh and bone. Spears pierced mail or boiled leather breastplates, axes hewed off arms or heads, swords stabbed through ringlets of mail to find the softer flesh underneath and the sound of shields smashing and clattering into each other and the sound of cold howling wind.

These Northmen were strong and were taking a heavy toll on the Medregorian numbers. Bargavon and the Northman lord traded blows. His sword was not finding a good angle on the giant's mailed torso and the ax was parrying the slashes to arms and head. In addition, his giant of an opponent seemed quite jovial, laughing and spouting off what might have been Northman taunts or funny insults. It must have been humor because a mailed Northman warrior laughed along with him as he drove an ax deep into a Medregorian soldier nearby. Meanwhile, the battle ax of his opponent was battering his own shield. It was nearly becoming a crumpled useless piece of metal.

I don't believe a human being could hit any harder if he tried. Bargavon's arm was starting to numb out and holding the nearly useless shield up was becoming difficult. He would have liked to have said it was weather related, but he knew the ax blows were reverberating off the shield and up his arm. The Northman lord seemed to actually be enjoying the fight as if it were jolly entertainment. He continued to laugh and shout in his native tongue. This was contagious and other Northmen around him followed suit. It seemed to Bargavon they were toying with the Medregorians. Bargavon's quick glance about him revealed far more dead Medregorians than Northmen. *Who were these guys?*

This behavior did not rattle Bargavon, it only made him angrier and when he got angrier, it infused him with a dark maleficent cunning that luxuriated in the essence of battle and killing. The merciless Imperial training of soldiers made for effective killing tools for the great Medregorian Empire and sometimes blended with a born natural instinct made for an ideal match. Time always seemed to slow down for him. Of course, maybe his thinking and actions sped up, certainly it was an interesting state Bargavon never spent much time contemplating, only experiencing in the present. He parried the next ax blow with his sword and then drove his sword point directly down into the heavy boot of the Northman lord. It sunk through and Bargavon twisted the blade snapping bones apart, severing ligaments and tendons and causing full ruin of the foot itself. A second later when the full sensation of pain raced from foot to head, did the Northman falter and react by bending forward to clutch at his foot upon which time his face met the rim of Bargavon's crumpled and ruined shield. The bridge of his nose exploded in cartilage and blood. He then howled and arched back spraying the white landscape with an arc of crimson.

Bargavon followed step as the Northman stumbled back. He threw off the ruined shield and took his sword in both hands raising it over his head and thrusting down onto the large man. The sword point pierced the mailed chest of the giant and with Bargavon's weight drove deep down to the hilt.

123

Blood sprayed from the wound through the mail and blood coughed from his bearded face. His sword was wedged through him into the ground and he could not retrieve it. The Northman laughed and coughed blood choking out some words in his Northern tongue and laughed again pointing up to Bargavon as if he was being let in on a joke.

Bargavon stepped back to draw out his dagger. The Northman rose and started to pull out the sword out of his own chest. The giant seemed to be a little exasperated at the state of a full long sword piercing his body. He shook his head and coughed out another blood-filled laugh. *By the Ninety-nine gods! Who is this ice demon from the North!?*

Bargavon did not want to be struck by his own sword after what he thought was a killing blow to his opponent and quickly looked about spying the ax dropped by the Northman. He quickly grabbed it and raced forward before the other to fully pull out his own blade. The mailed giant gave up on the impaled sword and actually dodged Bargavon's ax swing and pivoted driving a heavy fist into the upper back of Bargavon. The blow was hard enough to crack ribs and drive away his breath for some moments.

Bargavon spun around and readied the ax. The Northman stood there again smiling through blood covered teeth, his red blond beard soaked crimson. He gestured his arms wide as if offering an easy shot, and then waved Bargavon to come on. Bargavon did so and the Northman's ax removed the head of its previous master in one clean stroke. The effect on the other Northmen was nearly instantaneous. A great cry arose from them and they began to retreat. A Northman some distance away blew on an ox horn after seeing his leader go down. A dozen or more similar sounds answered it. The Northmen retreated off into the snowy gloom.

Bargavon would later find out that the Northman leader he slew was none other than the near legendary King Gamall Bhloud. By way of killing him, the rest of the chieftains following him lost heart and the entire Northman army fled back to their homelands. Bargavon's deed was witnessed by many and he was credited for turning back the Northman tide and thus gained instant fame and glory. He was soon advanced to the rank of captain and given his own company.

Over the next few years Bargavon and his company were involved in two major campaigns and several other battles, many of which earned he and his company recognition and fame. He was eventually attached to Army Group Eagle under General Targ, an older experienced general who allowed Bargavon's career to flourish and find even more glory.

Bargavon relinquished his hold and sat back, his mind had returned to the present. He was once again in the hold of some vessel carrying a company of warriors somewhere beyond the Veil. In a place somewhere between dreams, nightmares, heavens, hells, the starry skies of the Universe and the vast voids in between. Big Red slipped the blade back in his scabbard and leaned back against the hull, his fierce blue eyes never leaving Bargavon's.

"How long have you known Big Red, or shall I call you Gamall Bhloud?" stated Bargavon with a measured coolness. *Am I going to have to fight this monster again on this side?*

Big Red split the icy silence with thunderous laughter. "The whole time you half blind Medregorian jackass! Since that run when we picked your sorry broken sandy ass off the desert floor!" Laughter came from over a dozen warriors who had quietly watched this drama play out with interest unbeknownst to Bargavon.

"Fucking Karma, man! I was a little displeased that an olive colored whelp like you cut my head off with my own ax. You dark little fucker! Well, when we came upon you, guess who helped carry you aboard. What happened back in the Dense is irrelevant between us now. That was an epic fight though. I should have given you more respect in Tondra Pass. Usually you little Medregorians splintered like kindling. You're a tough, mean little bastard Medregorian."

Big Blue turned and looked at him with his large rhino like face. His voice was serious as he held Bargavon's gaze. "Remember this lesson. There will come a time, for each and every one of us when a retrieval is so painful, so personal, so overwhelming that it takes all we have to overcome it. Big Red is making light of it now, but trust me, he wasn't pleased when we found you and he got called out to carry you back. Your time will come. They always do."

The other noted event happened away from the Company. One evening, his night wanderings brought him to mountainous area. The sky was dark and danger seemed to creep into the very air itself. From where Bargavon stood, he could see a narrow trail, the Dark Warrior was moving up it carrying something of weight and wrapped in his dark cloak. The Dark Warrior looked back and sat down the cloak with its contents upon a natural shelf. Bargavon could see something coming as spectral sepia colored light cast harshly from torches washed over the rocks. The Dark Warrior stood, reflecting none of it. He drew forth sword and ax, just as Bargavon would however a mirror opposite, within his right the ax and the left wielded the sword.

Up the rocky trail came warriors. These Bargavon recognized as Medregorian royal guards dressed in gold gilded mail and helms with purple horsehair plumes debased to some ochre color within the strange sepia light of the torches they carried. They drew forth swords and scrambled up the trail. Down came the Dark Warrior upon them, complete blackness of form, only the hint of glowing red eyes and cruel black weapons arcing downward upon his foes. A strange screeching rasp issued forth from it horrifying to hear. Black blades met sepia hued mail, helm, blade and body.

Bargavon could hear the sword of metal on metal and the crack of bone being splintered within. The screams of pain and suffering rent the sepia gloom. The royal guards were cut down like sheaves of wheat at the harvest. They were no match for the arc of ax and sword that rent armor, broke blade and bent away parries as if they were weeds blowing in the wind. The Dark Warrior trampled down upon felled bodies as he cleaved into the tightly packed mob. The battle carried downward to an open piece of ground. There stood the Prince of Medregor, Prince Zhihar surrounded by his last few guards. He was arrayed in his princely finery and ceremonial gold gilded armor. He held alight a torch casting harsh sepia light that almost blurred away all that fell near it and creating an impressive halo about the prince.

Here the Dark Warrior faltered in his attack. The prince commanded the last guards to kill the Dark Warrior and on they came. They fought hard against him, but they too fell to their doom leaving only the Prince and the Dark Warrior who kept to the edges of the harsh torchlight, seething its raspy howls of hate.

The Prince looked up and saw Bargavon upon the rocks and hailed him. "Captain Bargavon, Hero of the Medregorian Empire, will you not defend me against this vile evil?"

Bargavon strode down to the clearing drawing both his sword and ax. It was duty that called, duty to Medregor and to the royal family. Prince Zhahir was known as a despicable human being but it was Bargavon's duty to protect him. He was a captain of Medregor, trained since age ten. He knew no other way. This is what he did. This was who he was. *Defend the Empire, defeat her enemies and bring glory to great Medregor, for the Emperor and the people.* This thought, this creed was drilled into his very core. A faint voice like a distorted sound of metal on stone skimmed across his consciousness *"Do not let him use you like a slave. What were you before?"*

He stepped into the Sepia light between the Prince and the Dark Warrior. His weapons were drawn, a mirror image of his dark self-pacing back and forth at the edge of the light.

"Step away. Only you and I have business." Announced Bargavon resolutely

The Dark Warrior coughed out a raspy laugh and pointed with his sword to the prince behind Bargavon, "That...is our business!"

Bargavon looked back at the prince and then back to the shadow prowling the edge the torchlight. "I don't understand."

"There is nothing to understand."

"Drive it off, Captain Bargavon. It is a vile cancerous thing that craves ill sought relevance and worth. It dooms your greatness. Slay it once and for all," Ordered the prince.

With the sepia light at his back Bargavon strode forth and the Dark Warrior retreated up the rocky steps until he reached the ledge whereupon there was a young boy holding something within the Dark Warrior's cloak that was draped across a rock. It was here the Dark Warrior retreated no more and with sudden power and violence surged against Bargavon whom parried away the ferocious blows. They were equals in combat and it seemed both warriors swung and parried, dodged and feinted against each other in equal measures. The clash of blades rang out clear in the strange light, held aloft behind Bargavon by the prince who followed him up the trail.

Suddenly, the Dark Warrior lost his footing and fell onto his back. Bargavon fell upon him with both sword and ax, the prince urging him on from behind. The Dark Warrior crossed his weapons above him locking and hooking Bargavon's own. Bargavon pressed his weight downward to break the bridge of black shadowed steel. The face of his adversary was black as midnight inches from his own face. The red glow of narrowed eyes and the sharp toothed grimace of the shadow so close to his own, the haggard hollow breath that escaped it sounded like grating of roughened stone and cracking ice.

"Nothing....to understand..." croaked the Dark Warrior, its red gaze releasing Bargavon's own and drifted past to the prince behind him, "remember...what he did!"

The sudden bark of a dog startled Bargavon out the momentary stalemate. The dog Valor seemed to have arrived on the stony path from nowhere. The distraction was all the Dark Warrior needed to quickly pivot underneath Bargavon and drive the haft of his ax under the chin of Bargavon. He staggered back choking and barely parried away a follow up swing by his opponent's sword.

In a brief moment, the Dark Warrior rushed up the natural steps to grab up both the boy and the cloak and blend into the vast darkness. Bargavon quickly recovered but his opponent had fled. The prince was safe. He turned but the prince was no longer there, nor the sepia light, nor the bodies of the guards, only Valor wagging his tail and sniffing about.

"I suppose you have a good reason for showing up here when you did?" said Bargavon plopping down upon a rock and scratching the dog's head. Valor said nothing, he was a dog and he didn't seem capable of speech, or if he was, he kept it to himself.

Chapter 8

The Battle of Wuxano

The city of Wuxano lay before them, a port city upon the Sudarian Sea. Wuxano was once part of the Medregorian Empire many years ago but won its freedom after several bloody battles. Up until today it was a trading partner and enjoyed a peaceful existence with its more aggressive Imperial neighbor. Someone had told Bargavon the Wuxani were forming an alliance with the Rukuse city-states, the Sudrasubian Kingdom and the Jarduse. He doubted this highly and most likely it was a well devised Imperial power grab with many nefarious political intrigues behind the scenes.

Privately over the last several months his view on the empire he served began to dim. His work beyond the Veil had been giving him perspective of life back here in the Dense. The Wuxani and Medregorians were essentially the same people, with the same gods, social and political structures and even royal bloodlines. This was a deep-seated family dispute and it was played out with the blood of both their loyal subjects.

In the past a new campaign and battle excited him. He personally enjoyed the thrill of battle and the glory. It gave him the opportunity to use his strategic command skills and put his combat skills to the test. The Imperial army gave him ample opportunity for this and he was very good at his craft. With all that was transpiring with his dual existence he was beginning to see the unnecessary drama in the petty wars and violence that took place here in "the Dense" as one of his warriors beyond the Veil called it. He was beginning to be conscious of his own actions, his own thoughts but here under the blazing sun and blue skies, here in this world he still had his obligatory part to play. Karma or not, he had not found a way out yet.

He stood upon the deck of a troop transport, next to him the ship's captain. Bargavon had under his personal command ten companies riding in this and the surrounding transport ships nearby. He and his lieutenant each had a company of eighty soldiers consisting of light and heavy foot as well as a squad of archers onboard this ship. These men could be seen down in the cargo hold busking for battle. The troop transports were designed to disembark troops quickly up several ramps from the cargo holds, unto the deck and off quickly deployable deck ramps and gangplanks. The sailors could deploy heavy hide screens on deck to partially shield the troops as they mustered to disembark. This was just one of about three hundred such troop transports that would deploy troops literally right onto the docks or seawalls of the city. Another force of Medregorians landed the previous day a few miles down the coast to lay siege to the western gate drawing at least some of Wuxano's forces away from the docks.

A few hundred yards ahead, Medregorian and Wuxani warships were clashing. Hails of arrows as well as catapult and ballistae artillery had already damaged several vessels on both sides, hundreds of sailors and marines lay dead on galley decks. Now, they were upon each other, ship rams smashing oar banks or metal clad reinforced prows gouging gaping holes in wooden hulls of their opponents. The sounds of splintered hulls, snapping oars, whining groans of buckling deck planks and hull timbers rent the air complemented by the roar of thousands of men and the shrill screams of agonizing deaths.

The Wuxani were putting up a hell of a fight thought Bargavon but Medregor was the premier superpower in the region. This one Imperial fleet alone was more than twice that of the entire Wuxani force. Wuxani skill in battle was admirable but numbers won out. The troop transports pushed past the remnants of the initial clash. The water was filled with dead bodies, splintered wood, broken oars, overturned and sinking vessels and blood. The sharks would soon be in to clean up.

The Medregorian warships reformed and began closing on the shoreline. Their decks filled with archers firing volleys of black arrows, their deck catapults firing a steady barrage of heavy shot and incendiary rounds lighting up the docks and waterfront with patches of fire and black smoke. The Wuxani knew the Medregorians would land here and returned fire with their own volleys of arrows and catapult fire. Their catapults however were land based and larger. Heavy stone shot fell among the ships sending up huge geysers of water, one landed just yards off the starboard side of their ship, spraying seawater across the deck. The transport just in front of them took a direct hit in the middle. The stone probably crushed a score of men on its way to punching a huge hole through the bottom of the hull, the force so strong it splintered and folded up the support timbers and the ship looked as if it was made of paper and folded in the middle. Water quickly engulfed it, many of its crew and troops heading under with it.

The transport was coming into shore. The captain angling the ship to come alongside a stone jetty. Already some of the marines were setting up the protective hide screens and just in time as dozens of arrows started falling around the ship. A couple sailors went down each with a few shafts in them. One arrow cracked and broke against the top of Bargavon's steel helm. The ship captain looked at him for a moment in wonder. Bargavon turned and gave a laugh, imbuing a sense of invincible confidence among his men.

That was fucking close. Another inch and that arrow would have been embedded in my eye socket and I would be permanently embedded with the Company beyond the Veil. Bargavon looked down upon the men crowded on the deck, pounded his mailed chest and roared out "Bring it you Wuxani whore-children! Wait no longer Medregorians! Your thirsty swords will soon feast!" He drew and raised his own sword as he said this for dramatic effect, his men readied themselves on the deck.

The gangplanks and assault ramps crashed onto the jetty. Bargavon was at the head of the first squad. Arrows from both sides crowded the air as men armored in chainmail and scalemail, carrying shield, spear and sword thundered across the platforms onto the jetty. The Wuxani footmen were ready with spear and shield to repel them. The initial crash of men was always the most exhilarating for Bargavon for it carried with it the last exhalation of anticipation and possibilities before the hand to hand combat dictated the outcome. Yells and screams rent the air, both of battle cries, as well as cries of wounded men. Bargavon always led with his most heavily armored troops, men in chain or scale mail with helms set with full faceguards, steel reinforced shields, heavy spears and longswords. These were his hand-picked men for their size as well. All were six feet or taller and were men of excellent bone and muscle structure. Medregorians and Wuxani were mostly average of height and tended to be around five foot eight inches, so these men were definitely on the large end of the spectrum. Bargavon used their massive size to intimidate as well as clear a gap for the rest of his squads.

Spear, shield, sword, flesh and bone all connected along the packed line at the edge of the jetty. The Medregorian footman next to Bargavon took a spear thrust well placed through his face guard demolishing flesh, bone and brain thus permanently preventing further life capability. Bargavon himself turned away two spear thrusts with his shield before twisting sideways to slide in among the Wuxani spearmen. His longsword held close and piercing forward between a gap in his opponent's brigandine armor, finding a few ribs and then some internal organs to slice through. The Wuxani's partner next to him turned to assist his fellow only to toppled by a downward longsword slice by one of Bargavon's heavy's. Within a half- minute the first squad drove into the Wuxani front line and cleared space for the rest of the squads to follow.

Bargavon worked his heavy squad through the front ranks and into the less packed second defensive line. More spaced out than the first, made up of militia troops most likely with a smattering of army regulars to hold them together. This is where they also placed their archers. Lieutenant Malibar's first and second squads also broke through about the same time and were barreling quickly into the second Wuxani line. The archers fired point blank into the armored wall that was crashing over them. Most of their shaft splintered against metal, a couple of Malibar's men along with one of his own were felled, but whether they were just wounded or dead was not up for contemplation at this time. Bargavon could see these men facing him were wide eyes and probably inexperienced. They could see that doom was about to fall upon them.

His sword took the head off the first man, his scared expression remained on his face as it sailed off into the melee. A second made a poor attempt at a spear thrust low which Bargavon deflected with his sword and followed that up with an upward thrust of his shield. It's top edge demolishing the man's mouth and sending teeth skittering across armor and stone. He did not have time to mourn their loss as a quick thrust through his quilted jerkin put an end to that. These troops were melting away as the metal clad wave of Medregorian Imperial troops smashed through. To either side two more transports were unloading troops, their resistance was much less as Bargavon was the point unit.

A few moments of rest brought Lieutenant Malibar over. "Captain Bargavon, too easy." He smiled but it was a grim smile, one practiced from many combat situations.

"Aye, Lieutenant. Let's move to the rendezvous point to meet up with General Targ, but stay alert, I'm sending several squads up a few streets to flank us. I want to make sure the Wuxani aren't using the buildings to screen a flanking force." replied Bargavon waving over his sergeants. He gave them quick orders and the companies moved double time down the jetty toward an area where the rest of the battle group was landing.

Halfway down to the rendezvous point, and about two hundred yards away, six companies of Medregorians of Battlegroup Eagle were forming up to move into the city. These were under direct command of General Targ. Bargavon made up the remainder the companies in this battle group although two hundred men were now under sea water, after taking the well placed trebuchet hit upon their vessel in front of Bargavon earlier.

Bargavon could see a sudden brief hail of arrows and javelins fall upon the packed mass of Targ's men, no doubt quite a few found a mark. Then from behind a line of buildings came the rush. The Wuxani waited for the Medregorians to form up before making a surprise counter-attack of massed pike men. These soldiers were Wuxani trained regulars, armed with long 14' pikes and arrayed in phalanx formations to present a nearly impenetrable wall of piercing spear points. They came quickly at the Medregorian battle group still trying to form up and caught them exposed.

Dozens of men went down pierced through with deadly effect. The Wuxani slowed from the impact and started what could only be described as a slow, death churn as each subsequent rank of pikes found new bodies to lance through. Their counter-attack was not without risk for they initiated it without fully securing their left flank. Only a screen of some archers and light javelineers were all that stood between them and Bargavon's companies of Medregorian footmen.

"Smash a hole through the line!" bellowed Bargavon, a grim smile upon his face for he smelled a route. The Wuxani may have caught General Targ flat footed but in so doing gave a free open shot to two nearly eight full Medregorian companies hitting their left flank and to Bargavon's delight three squads of light foot and one heavy foot that was sent out as his protective flank had come in from behind the Wuxani and caused them sudden distress. One of Bargavon's sergeants winded a battle horn. It sounded the arrival of aid, and the Medregorians being steamrolled by the great packed mass of deadly pikes rose up in a chorus of battle cries and one of them winded a horn in response.

The Wuxani screening archers and javelineers few in number and lightly armored if at all lost their shafts and braced themselves for their last few seconds on earth. In a moment a crash of metal, spear and sword swept them aside and under boot or sandal. The Wuxani pike men were trained men and given a short span of time, would have swept their left ranks into a pike bristling guard but they did not have that time given to them. The Medregorian heavy foot smashed into their flank and opened a great wedge. These pike men were armored only in leather jerkins and helmets, their pikes were both their attack and defense. Most had a side arm such as a long dagger or short sword, but they were packed close and weapons were hard to draw out, pikes were being dropped. In that packed space they had further impedance to mobility. The flank that was caving in no longer gave support to the front facing pike ranks and so the whole formation of hundreds of men began to implode.

At the center of the Wuxani implosion, Bargavon swung his sword in wide arcs trying to clear a space. No matter where he swung, his sword cleaved into arm, shoulder, face, neck and torso. Leather jerkins provided little stopping power to his longsword swung by powerful chorded muscles of his arms and shoulders. A few tried to stab at him with short sword or dagger, some were caught by his shield, some parried by his blade and a few just glanced against his mail. Although, at one point he was sure one penetrated his links and buried into his stomach, but the mail held. He was sure to have a nasty contusion and maybe a small cut as a reminder that he was always one lucky or well-placed strike away from calling it a life.

His men formed a cutting wedge behind him piercing through the pikemen ranks. To his left the Medregorians initially gored by pikes began hammering through gaps in the pike block. The route was beginning to happen. The Wuxani broke and streamed back dropping their heavy pikes, no longer useful in the close crush of this melee. Bargavon's men to their rear took further account of their numbers.

Heaps of dead and dying men packed together, lying about in blood, gore and broken pike shafts. The Medregorians had a moment to regroup. General Targ made his way to Captain Bargavon, stepping over dead bodies as he came. "By the Ninety-Nine, Captain Bargavon, you came in the nick of time!" hailed the general clasping Bargavon by the shoulders. "We heard their pikemen were at the Western Gate, not here unless they put to field more units than our recon were unaware of. Well done with that maneuver, Captain."

"Thank you, General." He and the general had a moment to survey the immediate field of battle. "On to the Battery Keep, General?" inquired Bargavon looking past the immediate buildings to a tall and wide tower not one hundred yards away behind a row of warehouses and wharf buildings. Behind the crenelated battlements, heavy stone shot fired out into the harbor at regular intervals. Their gaze tracked the heavy stones arcing out and bombarding the Medregorian ships still landing troops along the wharf, jetty and also on what piers were still serviceable.

"Ah, yes Captain, we will continue with the attack plan. Proceed with the assault on the tower battery. The siege engineers have just disembarked with the rams, and ladders. I have called up six more companies as well," Targ nodded to three transports unloading more troops as well as a company of siege engineers and all their equipment. "We start the attack in five minutes," stated General Targ, an expression of supreme confidence upon his face.

In that brief period of time Bargavon quickly met with his officers, most were still alive, one was killed at the initial jetty charge. Of his personal company of eighty, sixty-seven were still in fighting shape, the rest either dead or too wounded to fight. Another seventeen soldiers found their way to his company, remnants from another company that was decimated by trebuchet and flaming pitch that hit their transport upon reaching the jetty. Indeed, Bargavon could see the burning ruins of three ships at the jetty.

The second phase of the Wuxani assault called for the attack on the stronghold that contained the heavy batteries bombarding the ships in the harbor. The stronghold's walls were of stone and quite high. A main gate would have to be forced and he knew it would be well protected. This was a prospect he was not particularly looking forward to. He knew he was given this task because of his reputation. The casualties to his men would be great. Bargavon however prepared for this task. A month before when he learned of the Wuxano assault, he had done his own research on the fortifications here. Unlike other commanders, Bargavon did not solely trust his superior's knowledge or execution, so he often times would spend some of his personal resources to ascertain knowledge of his upcoming foe. He studied everything about them prior to a campaign. What were they like, what arms and armor did they use, what tactics they used, why did they fight and how was their psyche? If it were a location, he would try and buy maps or research maps in the archives. He would study them and try to memorize them. He would pretend he was there and visualize what it might look like; the terrain, the features, the climate, the elevation, the barriers, etc. He had the money to spend on these things for it was his passion, his career, his life and his men's lives at stake. The Empire paid him well enough and his defeated enemies seemed to give up more than enough looted treasure to satisfy him. Today, he knew that Targ requested a full out assault at the gate, which was unfortunate because his research told him that there was a rather well hidden sally port on the north end of the tower. It could be well defended but if forced through could give the Medregorians the advantage they needed. It was even conceivable that Wuxani didn't even have it guarded.

"Get me Malibar quickly!" ordered Bargavon to one of his sergeants. "I have a plan." *We will succeed in taking this tower, but not how Targ thinks we will by throwing hundreds of men to their deaths pushing through a contested gate,* thought Bargavon, pulling out his own hand-drawn map of the fortifications he had copied from the archives.

The battlegroup approached the tower in good order. They kept back out of site of the battlements to avoid getting pin cushioned by dozens of archers waiting above. Down the street from the main gate, the assault engineers had loaded the prebuilt hide covered gallery onto the wheeled undercarriage. Hanging in the gallery was an iron shod ram hung from chains to allow it to swing. A score of men would be under the gallery to both move it to the gate and then operate the ram. The hide coverings were layers thick and soaked with water to make them fireproof. Wheeled ballistae would lay covering fire along with a company of archers. The assault engineers were also providing them movable mantlets, wooden walls on wheels that the archers could move forward under cover and then fire volleys of arrows from. Small catapults called onagers were brought from the ships to lay down harassing fire against the battlements.

When all was set, General Targ gave the order to commence the attack. Onagers from five different locations launched rock and incendiaries up toward the battlements lighting them up. Ballistae down the street from the gate fired flaming heavy javelins and flaming pitch filled clay canisters at the wooden gate to set it ablaze. A half charred door would be weakened and allow better penetration by the ram.

Bargavon set the plan in motion that he had discussed earlier with his lieutenant. He left the main body of his troops with lieutenant Malibar and took three squads of men around the north side of the keep and kept to the street behind a section of buildings. Some of these men were borrowed assault engineers armed with portable two-man rams made of iron shod oak and heavy pry bars, the rest were many of his most experienced soldiers.

Lieutenant Malibar sat waiting with the main assault force. The gate was on fire and he was letting it burn to make shorter work for the ram. Occasional missile fire rained down into his men. The Wuxani were arcing it over the roofs blindly. Occasionally, one found a mark as this part of the street was packed thickly with Medregorians ready to storm the breach.

Meanwhile to the north, Bargavon peered around the corner of a boarded up tavern. They were directly across from what should be the sally port. There were a few wooden shacks built up against the tower on the north side; buildings best described as a small merchant stalls and food stalls. One directly in front looked like a food stall and behind it was stacked several large barrels. The area was empty of people, because they had probably cleared out many hours ago. He looked up to the battlements. Only a couple of men were watching high above on the wall. Their attention was mostly to the west where the main battle was. Hopefully, by the time Bargavon broke through the sally port, their alarm would be too late. He turned and signaled that there were two guards above. Five of his men had bows and rushed out from under the eaves of the tavern roof and loosened a volley up at the guards. One of them took a couple arrows in his chest and head and fell from view, one of the other three arrows sunk into the neck of the other guard who jerked about uncontrollably for a moment while reaching for the feathered shaft impaled through his neck.

Bargavon led his first squad across the street and into the empty food stall. Behind it they found stacked barrels which they rolled away to reveal a stout iron banded oak door. The assault engineers got to work smashing it and prying at it with their tools. Behind them and across the street Bargavon's archers were staying alert for other guards to appear above on the wall.

"Almost got it Captain," said an engineer through gritted teeth as his two-man pry bar loosened an iron door hinge. A moment later, they pried out the door and Bargavon led the attack inside. It was immediately dark compared to the bright sunlight of the day. They found themselves in a narrow passageway. It was empty. *Must be a trap laid for us*, thought Bargavon. With weapon in hand, he half crouched his way with quiet haste up the passage. A dim light outlined a door. It opened to what may be a mustering chamber. The door they had come through was hidden behind an old dusty tapestry and apparently had not been used for some time. The chamber was bare and had but one door and was lit only though a partially opened door that appeared to open out into a sunlit courtyard. *Incredulous!* thought Bargavon not believing his luck. *Did they forget they had this portal or did someone simply forget to defend it?* Men running about the open yard within the keep could be seen from their hidden location.

Bargavon turned to his men crouched in the darkness. He could see the occasional glint of mail or steel boss of a shield. Their breaths were quick and shallow with anticipation. "Alright, find a way to the top of the gate and try to disrupt the defenders over it."

Speed and surprise was of the essence. Bargavon burst forth into the wide courtyard. The gate was at the west end and above it the massive gatehouse. A mass of troops of at least a couple hundred men were preparing to plug up the breech should the gate be smashed down. He could see squads of troops pouring buckets of water on the smoking door, he was sure the front side was alight with fire arrows and burning pitch. Several ballistae bolts were pierced halfway through the heavy wood as well. To the south of the courtyard, three great trebuchets were firing massive stones out into the harbor, behind them up on the keep battlements, spotters were calling down coordinates. Two men rolling a water barrel toward the gate passed in front of the Medregorians bursting from their hiding spot. The second it took them to realize they were not Wuxani soldiers gave enough time for them to be cut down.

"Stairs!" bellowed Bargavon pointing his longsword to a set of stone steps leading up to a parapet that ran toward the gatehouse.

They sped across the side of the courtyard knocking over or cutting through any Wuxani in their way. Behind them up upon the battlements of the keep, they heard an alarm and the sound of bows twanging. Bargavon charged up the steps, his sword sweeping out in front of him in wide arcs sending bodies tumbling off or dropping in place only to be run over by Medregorian heavy footmen. Most of the Wuxani here were carrying supplies such as arrows, oil, rocks and other projectiles up to the top to drop upon the enemy storming the front gate. At the top, Wuxani soldiers were alerted to the fast approaching strike force. They dared not launch spear, javelin or arrows into them for fear of hitting their own men still upon the stairs struggling to get clear. They instead waited with spear, shield and drew forth swords.

A spear thrust, and a sword blow simultaneously hit Bargavon in his own shield and across the faceguard of his helm causing a momentary blinding flash of pain. His own sword sliced horizontally in front cutting above a greave armored leg and dropping the spear wielder in his place, his lower quadriceps now detached from his knee. His opponent with the sword took a spear through the chest by one of his own men behind him. This was a mad rush and he did not have time to be slowed upon an exposed stairway. He and his front ranks lowered themselves behind their shields and continued to lunge forward, pressing the defenders back. Bargavon's second and third ranks were using their spears, much like the Wuxani phalanx pike men from earlier. Men died to either side of this contested front but Bargavon's momentum carried him and his squads securely up upon the battlements of the gatehouse.

The defenders had their own ballistae and squads of archers returning fire down the street at the Medregorian assault waves. There was the smell of burning oil, but he did not see it, perhaps a floor below, just over the gateway thought Bargavon, ducking behind his shield as a couple archers turned their attention toward him. Barring some losses, he still had close to three squads with him, most of these heavy footmen including his personal 'Heavies.'

The Wuxani here numbered close to the same but they were much lighter armed and armored. They were ballistae operators and archers, few had anything more than a leather jerkin or quilt jacket on, some had helmets, some did not and only a few had shields at the ready. The Medregorians fell about in wild melee. Their heavier swords, spears and hand axes wrought death and ruin upon the defenders that up until a minute ago enjoyed a birds-eye view of the battle and were picking off the Medregorians on the street with near impunity.

Identifying an officer, Bargavon moved to engage him. The man was also dressed in chainmail and had grabbed up a shield as well. The two met in a clash of swords and shields. Bargavon was using a heavier long sword for the battle while the officer was carrying the wide bladed short sword that was typical of the region. Having a longer reach gave Bargavon that advantage of landing two blows into arm and shoulder while deflecting away his opponent's first strikes. The officer swung a long kick that tripped up Bargavon and sent him backward. A series of fast sword thrusts were narrowly deflected by both sword and shield before. Blood was seen dripping down the arm of the officer. Bargavon's first blows had caused more damage than he had thought. He noticed the officer was thrusting and was avoiding overhead movement with his sword arm. After a few feints, Bargavon swung down toward the top of the man's sword arm and shoulder. His opponent couldn't bring his arm up to a high guard and parry in time.

Bargavon's sword almost took the arm off had it not been for his enemy's chain armor. He went down in a heap, and Bargavon followed with downward stab above his collar ending his life.

A quick survey of the situation told him that his men were securing the top of the gatehouse. Bargavon took a moment to look over the side at the gate below. The assault engineers had already rolled up the covered gallery to the gate and started ramming. The hide covered gallery was pincushioned with scores of arrows and a few holes showed that dropped rocks or a heavy bolt made their way through it.

There was a floor below the roofline that probably had a murder hole from which the defenders could pour burning oil down on the attackers that would soon be pressing through the gate. He could see heavy rocks, spears and some bow fire coming also from the floor below. His sergeant called to him that they found the stairway down into the gatehouse. He quickly made his way there, about him small pockets of resistance were being mowed down by his men. At the top of the stairs his first squad formed, seven of his original twelve men were ready along with two siege engineers and his sergeant.

They rushed downward into the second level. The main room did indeed have a cauldron of burning oil hanging from a movable rig and operated by chains over a murder hole which looked down upon the entrance passage. The Wuxani had a second cauldron being heated nearby and was on a track to slide over and take the place of the first once it dropped its deadly rain of burning oil. About twenty men were here, half were archers or soldiers dropping debris out the forward facing windows and arrow slots. The rest were soldiers

147

preparing the oil and ready for the orders. Another officer was here with his attention on the murder hole waiting for the moment the Medregorians poured into the entrance passage. Bargavon could hear the gate breaking apart, wood splintering and groaning against the thud of an iron shod ram. It would be less than a minute. The Medregorians wasted no time and fell upon the defenders.

The officer turned at the sound of yelling men and the sudden chaos, he drew forth his sword as Baragvon leaped to attack. He was quick and his skill at arms was quite good. For several moments, he and Bargavon dueled with swords in a series of feints, parries and crossing swords. He did not have a shield and Bargavon made use of his own by battering him backward over the body of a dead Wuxani soldier. As he fell back, Bargavon's sword drove through the links of ringmail he wore and deep into his torso. Around him the Wuxani fought fiercely but these were Bargavon's best troops and his foes were outmatched in skill, arms and armor.

The last of the defenders were either killed or too wounded to fight, so Bargavon ordered a few men to remain in the room to prevent the oil cauldrons from falling back in the Wuxanis' hands. Bargavon and several men moved the oil cauldrons away from the murder hole just before the gate came crashing down. From his position above, Bargavon could see the first wave of Medregorians pouring through. A few volleys of arrows from Wuxani in the courtyard made sure not all of them made it past the gate.

"The rest of you with me!" commanded Bargavon heading back to the parapet. From there he could see the Medregorians smashing into the Wuxani defenders in the courtyard. It would soon be a morass of packed men swinging at each other with no sense of tactical formation. However, the trebuchet crews bolted for the safety of the keep and so the main goal was accomplished. The ship demolishing rain of rocks had ended.

Upon the parapet, the Medregorians encountered defenders and several minutes were spent clearing them. The courtyard below was a packed mass of swords, spears, armored men, flashes of crimson spray, and a discordant chorus of battle cries, screams, bellowing orders and death. Bargavon forced his way through a well-defended doorway and into the keep. His original strike squads were bolstered by several more squads from his personal company as they gained access into the keep proper. What followed was almost an hour of close hand to hand combat; quick deadly room clearing battles interspersed by minutes spent forcing open doors and other obstacles to gain access to the rooms. In the end, Bargavon took the keep, while his Lieutenant took the courtyard. The landings of the second and third waves out in the harbor were free of trebuchet fire as the Medregorian flag was hoisted above the tower for both sides to see.

Over the next few hours, the remainder of the Medregorian army landed in Wuxano and a day of fierce street battles ensued. Bargavon's company saw more action and was credited for taking several of the arched bridges that webbed through the city's intricate canal system. By the end of the second day, the remaining Wuxani had fled, fought to the death in fierce pockets of resistance or surrendered. The Medregorians then went about securing the city.

On the third day after taking the city, Bargavon led a squad down one of the winding cobblestone streets. This quarter of the city was relatively quiet of violence and some locals were starting to venture out and try to reclaim part of their lives. After all that was done, to the Medregorians, it was a simple change of government, not a destruction of the Wuxani way of life. Tradesmen and shop keepers cautiously began to open a few businesses. Old men and women too slow to escape the city began to peer out from window or stand at their front doors watching the Imperial troops patrol by. One tavern owner nearby was calling to the soldiers to come in for a drink. Serving Imperial troops may be a lucrative move. After all this was to be a reclaimed Imperial city, therefore the tavern owner bet that the troops would pay their silvers and coppers instead of tear the place up unlike a foreign kingdom or city.

There was some activity going on just beyond a partially covered doorway. Outside the building several wounded Wuxani soldiers were either lying or sitting with their backs against the white stucco wall. They were dressed in fresh bandages. A young boy was moving among them offering water from a clay flask. These beaten men eyed the Medregorian soldiers wearily.

"Boy, what is beyond that doorway," commanded Bargavon. His men needed no direction as they fanned out with swords drawn looking for any possible ambush. The boy stated that a healer was taking care of some of the wounded men and that they would not be any trouble.

Bargavon entered the building with three of his men, their swords drawn. It took a moment for his eyes to adjust from the bright noon sun to the oil lamp lit interior. The place may have been a neighborhood café or tavern. There were some long tables and benches upon which lay several more wounded men. A Wuxani healer and two more assistants were tending to some wounded as well as dying soldiers. Bargavon said nothing as he walked among the wounded and dying. He had done these walks many times after battles.

Men of all races, nations and cities pretty much look the same at this stage. The fight has gone out of most. Some pray to their gods, others crying out for family members either alive or dead, some just moan incoherently and most ask for water, even if they end up coughing it all back out. It is a messy scene and something that always seems left out of the victorious war stories. Bargavon knew at this moment field hospitals were being set up by his people and similar scenes were playing out there.

The Wuxani healer moved to place himself before Bargavon and held up his palm "Kill me, if you must Medregorian, but I will not allow you to harm or harass these men. Leave them in peace. They have given their life and limb against you." Although a man of healing, he was passionate and protective of the men left in his charge.

"Healer, I mean to cause no further harm, we are securing this quarter." Something seemed peculiar out of the corner of his eye in the corner as soon as he finished. There was something wrong with the shadows in a corner near a dying man who was delirious and babbling incessantly. It was as if the shadows flickered or moved a bit, but this seemed out of place with the rest of the light and shadows the other oil lamps cast.

"Medregorian, I must insist you leave so I can return to my work!" demanded the healer but Bargavon's interest drew to this corner of the room.

He never took his eyes away from the man in the corner as he answered, "If you continue your yapping healer, I will run you through with my blade and you will be sorely missed by those unfortunates left here bereft of your service."

Something like a faint shadow ran up the corner then back down, another seemed to be just sitting at the end of the table the man was sprawled on. When Bargavon focused on these shadowy forms they disappeared, only to reappear at his peripheral vision. A cold tingle went up his spine. He felt he was being watched by menacing eyes. His hand twitched reflexively as if begging to unsheathe his sword.

He was now looking down at the dying Wuxani soldier. He had an abdominal wound and it was wide and deep. Hasty bandages were already soaked with blood and pulling away to reveal his insides. The man was feverish and babbling about demons surrounding him, grabbing at him, waiting for him to die so they could have him. His eyes were glazed over, but he turned and faced up at Bargavon. "Please help me, drive them off, they are so close to me!" his speech trailed off into garbled hisses and grimaces of horrible pain. Something passed over the man's face just then, a faint translucent shadow, so quick and ephemeral that Bargavon blinked thinking it was his eyes tricking him. His hairs stood up on the back of his neck. All his combat senses were now on full readiness, but nothing was there to fight. The feeling was almost overpowering, and he felt his hand now wrap around the hilt of his sword automatically. Suddenly, the man gasped and arched up, a guttural crackling issued from his throat then he expired. The feeling of an impending attack also ended at that moment as did the peripheral shadow movement. Bargavon looked down at the face of the dead man, still twisted in both agony and terror, eyes wide. He turned and looked away taking in the rest of the room. The healer was trying to sew up a head wound, his assistants were fetching water and towels, injured men lay on tables and his own men walked about with only mild interest in anything here. They were seasoned and seen all this before. No one except Bargavon appeared to have noticed any eeriness in the corner other than a delirious man dying, no other except perhaps the young water boy at the door. His wide eyes were fixed on Bargavon.

"Leave them, they are no threat anymore. Move out!" commanded Bargavon sharply and hastily made his way through the injured, the dead, the dying and directly toward the door and to the water boy. *He saw them too. Interesting*

Now outside in the hot bright sun, the strange corner activity seemed to him now as a trick of his imagination and he might have waved it off as such but for the water boy's response and his own frequent trips across the Veil. Bargavon grasped the boy by his arm quickly and carried him across the street and placed him on an abandoned cart.

"Start talking boy. What did you see!" the words came out of Bargavon a little more menacing than he meant but the shadow activity was reminiscent of dark predatory beings beyond the Veil. The fact that he could see interactions occurring between both worlds concerned him and interested him equally. The boy was quite frightened, either by what he saw or by Bargavon's own present menace. Eventually with some gentle prodding he relaxed enough to converse.

"I saw demons hunched around the man dying in the corner. They were pawing at him. I saw them pull at him when he died. It was like they yanked out his soul like a sheet and they all disappeared into the corner."

Bargavon gently placed his hand upon the boy's shoulder, as the boy started to shake and cry. After a few minutes Bargavon asked him if he had ever seen anything like that before. He had only a few times before, one was during the public execution of a criminal and the other happened to a dying Medregorian on the street earlier today.

"Why do you think you see these things? Do you have training or was your mother a witch?" inquired Bargavon, his interest deepening.

The boy nodded a little. "Last year I was sent to study with the clergy. I was an assistant for one of the priests. He often took me to strange rites underground in the catacombs or out in the hillside tombs. He never explained what he did, but he seemed to converse with things that were not there. His lantern always seemed to cast a strange light during these rites and the shadows always flickered funny. At first, I thought it was my imagination making them out to be silhouettes of people talking with him or dancing around, but now I know they were real. The priest spoke in a strange tongue and he never explained what was said. He always had me stand a ways behind him holding up a second lantern and just wait. He said to alert him if anyone approached. After he was done he would ask if I saw anything unusual or anyone and I would lie and say no."

"Is there anything else you can tell me boy, I need to know," inquired Bargavon.

"The shadows seemed to flinch from you, warrior. When you moved, they would avoid you. I don't think they liked you, maybe they were scared of you."

A shout from across the street broke Bargavon's attention from the boy, "Captain run me through if you feel it to be your duty, but I need that boy back inside tending to these men!" shouted the exhausted and increasing irritating healer from the doorway across the street. His bloodstained hands were on his hips holding a blood soaked rag

"Go boy, I have killed enough men for the last few days, and your master is just begging me to add another to my tally," smiled Bargavon clasping the boy's hands in his own and slipped him a silver coin "Thank you, young man." The boy smiled and quickly hid the coin in his tunic.

"Warrior, do you fight with those dark ones?" inquired the boy.

"Yes, but on a different battlefield far from here." Bargavon stated staring off nowhere in particular and absently scratched at the stubble on his chin as the boy nodded and then ran back across the street. *Is it possible both sides of the Veil are bleeding over into the other side or is it always that way and now I am more aware of it all?*

It was late in the day, and Bargavon's company was beginning to secure themselves a location to bivouac for the night. Bargavon had temporarily claimed a nobleman's dwelling for his own and his officers. Its previous occupants were probably hiding up in the foothills around Wuxano, fleeing with many of the population before the assault got underway. Bargavon sat in a low comfortable chair, drinking wine from the lord's fine silver goblets. He eyed the diamond ring he held in his hand. Its facets caught the candlelight close to it momentarily mesmerizing Bargavon with their scintillating beauty. *Krin will like this.* He had found it along with a cache of other jewelry, gold and silver coins in a strongbox in a hidden cellar chamber. Bargavon and his men had gotten quite good at locating loot over the years. Most people were predictable and this nobleman showed little ingenuity in hiding his wealth.

The room was dimly lit by a few lanterns with the wicks turned low. In the corner, the shadows seem to deepen and flicker. An unnatural flicker that was reminiscent of the dying Wuxani soldier earlier in the day. Bargavon watched them as he intently took slow sips from the goblet. "I see you. Be gone. I'll be asleep soon and perhaps I will mark your presence and come after you." Bargavon had lost his fear of supernatural things. He faced them nearly every night beyond the Veil in their own natural environment. He was amused that the shadows seemed to depart at his threat.

The next morning, Bargavon and his company spread out to patrol their quarter. Already some of the Wuxani citizens were coaxed back to the city by the lenient and 'gracious' attitude of Medregor. The city was under martial law and the Medregorians were strictly enforcing it.

Sudden yelling and screaming brought Bargavon and his two squads off the street and down a wide alley. Before him a squad of Imperial soldiers were clustered, many looking into a passage that led to a small courtyard. A sergeant tried to block Bargavon and recognizing him apologetically said, "Sorry Captain Bargavon, Royal business. Please turn and go back to your patrol. I insist on his Highnesses orders."

"There is no one from the royal family here in the Wuxano. Don't be ridiculous sergeant," Snapped Bargavon

"Please Captain, turn back around. I strong insist." The sergeant replied anxiously

The screaming rose higher and Bargavon pushed past the sergeant, who went to give the order to draw swords until one of Bargavon's sergeants put a blade to his neck and told him and his squad to stand down. Royal business or not, they were outnumbered two to one by Bargavon's men.

Bargavon left the soldiers to square off with each other in the alley, as he moved through the short passage to a small open air courtyard. A Medregorian man was bending a teenage girl over the courtyard's fountain edge. Three of his soldiers were holding a family at bay, a father, mother and two teenage girls. They were down on their knees begging and crying, spear points leveled at them. A couple blood covered bodies of young men nearby indicated perhaps sons or brothers that tried to resist.

Bargavon strode quickly across the cobblestone courtyard, a silvered chain shirt and a well- made, embossed helmet lay behind the man as he bent over the helpless girl. The insignia on his sash slung over his shoulder showed he was a captain. His sword was in its scabbard and propped up against the fountain edge next to him. One of the guards ordered Bargavon to stop and drew his sword. They met halfway and Bargavon ducked a poor swing of a longsword and smashed the pommel of his sword through the faceguard breaking a nose and putting the man into instant sleep. The commotion stopped the other Medregorian captain from carrying out his task with the Wuxani girl to turn defiantly at the offender. Bargavon never broke stride and punched him across the jaw sending him over into the fountain with a splash. The naked girl broke and ran. The other two soldiers guarding the family immediately leapt to defend their commander. Bargavon turned to face off with them. As they ran at him, one threw his spear that glanced off his shoulder and gave him a stinger down the left arm. The other had dropped his spear and drew his sword. As he came Bargavon kicked a bench into him, toppling him over. He ran over the top of this downed soldier to ring his blade off the helmet of the guard who threw the spear. The guard passed by and staggered for a second. Bargavon still atop the toppled soldier kicked him in the face removing a few teeth.

As the other soldier tuned and regained a fighting stance, Bargavon sprung upon him in a storm of sword blows, none of which were meant to kill the other Medregorian, only to disable him. He was no match for Bargavon and was soon backpedaling and fell over a table. A few of Bargavon's men rushed in to support their commander and held these men down at sword-point.

The captain whose attempted rape was so rudely interrupted by Bargavon stepped out from the fountain soaked in what little clothing remained. "I am prince Zhihar, first son of Emperor Zharzidan and I will see to your execution soldier!" screamed the officer livid with rage.

Kill him now! This is your chance. Our chance! Do it now! urged a sudden raspy scream in his mind. It was the voice of the Dark Warrior.

"You are in my sector captain and these people are under my direct jurisdiction!" commanded Bargavon sheathing his sword. "Restrain that officer, sergeant!" and his men quickly overtook the other captain and bound his wrists.

"You will die before me fool!" screamed the man.

"Gag him too. I do not want to hear his shrill voice anymore. We will take him to General Targ to sort this out" Bargavon's men chuckled as the captain claiming to be a prince was gagged and drug away.

The family had fled indoors except for the Wuxani father, a man in his late thirties who fell on his knees before Bargavon "Thank you, Captain, I am forever in your debt.

Please ask anything of me, but spare my wife and daughters." He was crying tears and had his hands clasped before him.

"Get up man, and bury your dead. I fear some of our men have not the discipline to understand any restraint. I can do no more for you except continue to offer my protection here while stationed in your sector." He then glared over at the officer being dragged away. He looked familiar, but Bargavon was sure he was no officer in his army group, perhaps another battle group. *I have seen that face before. There is a resemblance but Prince Zhahir should be safely tucked away in the palace at Kathvitora, there would be no reason for him to be here now.* He could feel something in his gut, an overpowering sensation of impending doom. A feeling that a dreadful turn of events was happening, and he was no longer able to escape its grasp.

As they exited the courtyard and into the alley, Bargavon could see an ashen look upon sergeant Rattik's face. The other squad they faced had stood down, but the sergeant that warned him initially of royal business was speaking angrily to Rattik and pointing into the courtyard. As Bargavon started to approach this officer and to see what Rattik seemed so concerned about, a clamor of more Medregorian soldiers poured into the alley surrounding him and his men, their weapons were drawn.

The angry officer and some of his men hastily removed the gag and bindings around the wrists of the captain. The captain was livid and pulled at his beard, tearing it completely off. It took only seconds for Bargavon to see he had made a mortal error. The beard was a disguise, behind it hid the prince, his eyes blazing death at Bargavon. "Seize him and take him away!"

Chapter 9

Everything Unravels & Becomes Clear

It was an hour after the courtyard rape incident. Bargavon found himself in General Targ's command center. It was the former Wuxani Harbor Master's Villa up until a few days ago. Bargavon was standing at attention. Before him was his commanding officer, General Targ, the man in charge of the entire assault, Field Marshall Vendana and what was now obvious as a screaming and stomping Prince Zhahir. *I did recognize the fucking bastard then, even with the stupid disguise. I should have just killed him when I had the chance and accepted the consequences. It would have been better that way. Perhaps, the Dark Warrior was right.*

The large room also contained several officers and personal assistants to the General staff. All seemed somewhat nervous. It appeared that the prince decided to dress up as a captain, so he could partake in the 'spoils of war'. *So he wanted to play warrior, without actually fighting and act out some sexual fantasy in a real war zone. I regret not killing the degenerate in the courtyard.*

A voice began to whisper in his head, a voice both familiar and ghostly. *Kill him and send him to Hell! You have been there. He deserves it and you know it. Do you remember now? Do you remember what he did to us? You still have a chance, you are so close to him and there are weapons within reach.* Sweat began to trickle down Bargavon's face and back. To those present it would seem he looked nervous concerning the significant trouble he was in, but that was not true. Inside he was pondering the voice he knew was from the Dark Warrior and not wanting to open up a memory, a deep wound he had covered up many years before. He willed himself not to crack, to reach back all those years and rip open the wound. Yes, he remembered now, Prince Zhahir was there, so was....*No! I am stronger than this and I will not let that memory control me!* His internal struggle was gratefully broken by the stern voices near him.

The Field Marshall spoke "Your Highness, I thought we discussed that you would arrive a week after we fully secured the city. It will be yours once we have everything restored in good order."

"We discussed it Vendana, but ultimately I decide where and when and how I go. You work for me Field Marshall, you run the army, you are not in charge of ordering around royal family members!" screeched the prince, getting into the taller and much bigger Field Marshall's face. He turned and pointed to Bargavon who remained outwardly stoic, only the sweat gave away any physical discomfort. He had twenty plus years of military service, being yelled at, yelled to or generally yelling yourself was as normal as breathing. "I want this man tortured and then executed for attacking a member of the royal family!"

General Targ carefully and slowly began to explain so as not to further agitate the prince who was quite nearly raving at this point "Pardon me your Highness, but my captain did not know who you were when he was investigating a disturbance in his sector. In the heat of the moment he....." He was cut off by the sound of alarm bells from the eastern and northern gates.

The prince ignored the sudden looks of confusion and alarm on his generals' faces and started to rant again when Field Marshall Vendana's voice boomed out "Please be quiet your Highness! Targ go see what that's about!"

General Targ sprinted to the balcony and looked out. He turned and shouted back, alarm in his voice "It's a massive counterattack. The Wuxani must have hidden a second army in the hills and it looks like they have gotten aid from abroad. There is Jardusii ships bearing down into the harbor!"

"Right, Gentlemen, send word out to the troops to muster for battle. Form up at the main square and the old palace. Targ, take your army group back into the harbor area, your stationed closest to that." ordered Vendana springing into action. Men began to scatter in a hurry as more alarm bells started to ring and mustering horns could be heard. The Medregorians were highly trained and seasoned. They could reform fighting formations and set up defensive positions second to none on earth.

"Wait! What about my justice. This man needs to be tortured and executed!" stammered the prince who looked about incredulous to the fact an event was interrupting his 'justice.'

"Ah yes, well your Highness, I have need of highly capable leaders at the moment, so I am going to borrow back Captain Bargavon for a little bit until I get this counterattack repulsed. Then, if he or even if we live, well, we will discuss it then. General Targ, get down to the harbor and take Captain Bargavon with you," ordered Vendana waving them off. Targ and Bargavon bolted down the steps, they had only minutes to get the companies reformed for battle. The sound of Prince Zhahir ballyhooing quickly subsided under the din of bells, horns and the sound of a trebuchet launching heavy rocks into the harbor.

"So glad we didn't damage those things. They will be coming in handy for us today," smiled Targ grimly as he ran next to Bargavon nearing the predetermined muster area. Already about half of the companies arrived and more men were streaming in from multiple streets, most still carrying their armor and gear.

"I will have to thank the Wuxani general for attacking when he did. Perfect timing," said Bargavon slowing his speed so Targ could keep up.

"Yes Captain, now if some stray Wuxani arrow or catapult shot could put an end to that pompous princeling's life, we will have that problem solved as well." replied Targ through his puffing breaths. "Go ahead to your companies without me, I'll be there shortly. This is why generals should be on horseback. We're too old for all this running around."

The counterattack by the Wuxani relief army and a mercenary naval force of Jardusii failed to retake Wuxano. The battle was brief and bloody but the Wuxani and Jardusii received the worse end of it. The men of Bargavon's company once again proved themselves admirable in combat as they sprung upon the Jardusii mercenaries landing on the jetties. Captain Bargavon himself fought the Jardussi mercenary commander. A dusky giant of a man donned in red lacquered armor and a great steel helm set with buffalo horns. He wielded a great two-handed sabre that had split more than a few Medregorians in half that day. Bargavon fought him smartly and drew him into an area where the wide arc of the Jardusii's swings were neutralized by the masts and rigging of a capsized galley next to the jetty. Bargavon kept working his longsword jabs to pierce the joint gaps in the thick armor. After several minutes, the blood loss was enough to slow the Jardusii commander down allowing Bargavon a quick decisive stab into a narrow gap near his throat. The dusky giant's knees buckled and Bargavon jumped onto him driving the sword downward through the neck and into the thoracic cavity killing him.

It was at the tail end of the battle as the last Jardussi were being repelled when one of General Targ's staff members ran up to him. Nearly breathless he relayed a message that he was to report at once to Targ's command post at the Tower Keep. Bargavon left Lieutenant Malibar in charge as he made his way there. He found General Targ at the rooftop tower surveying the harbor. Already the Jarduse naval vessels were withdrawing from the harbor, only pockets of mercenaries remained fighting along the wharf and one of the jetties. To the North and East fighting could be seen on the walls and near the gates but Medregorian flags still flew over these key points.

Targ turned to Bargavon and clasped him on both shoulders "My dear Captain Bargavon. It has been my honor to have you as my best commander all these years. I was going to recommend you for promotion to colonel after this campaign, but circumstances have dictated otherwise. You know I am ordered to turn you over to the Prince for your execution. He is an unscrupulous royal suckling of a weasel and I pray someday that court intrigue will lead to his poisoning or assassination. You are a hero, the finest commander a general could ever have and you have been loyal and faithful. I cannot bear your suffering and death for the whim of that whelp. I am sure Field Marshall Vendana feels likewise. That is why I am sad to report that you have been killed today. One of the trebuchet's accidentally hit a Jardusii ship that you and your men boarded near the jetty. Horrible way to go I'm afraid. Your body was crushed and recognizable only by your insignia."

Bargavon understood clearly, but said nothing. His twenty year military career just ended. Targ called over one of his assistants. Kojinn, please see that this marine before me here makes it on board the *Sunfire* before dusk. I believe it leaves tomorrow morning back to Kathvitora with some captured tribute. They are in need of another marine. Also send for Lieutenant Malibar, he will have to take over command for the recently killed Captain Bargavon." He turned back to Bargavon, a sad smile and then a reassuring nod "Marine, if I were you I would return and get my house in order. Perhaps take up farming or herding in a border province far away from the capital. Goodbye my friend." They clasped hands and then General Targ turned away as another assistant brought him recent updates from the other sectors in the battle.

Kojinn did not miss a beat "Follow me marine, we need to get you out of that armor and clothing and into something suitable for you. Barring any damage from the sea battle, the *Sunfire* awaits and we should get you there and on the roster." Bargavon just nodded solemnly and followed him down the stairs into the keep. There was a feeling of a chaotic free fall in his solar plexus. His life seemed to be imploding and the walls of the 'Dense' collapsing in on him.

That night a new marine was rostered aboard the *Sunfire*. He was shown a cramped place to stow his gear which amounted to not much more than a rucksack, his shield, helm, and a skin of watered wine. He settled in for the night, his mind was quite unsettled however.

Bargavon awoke before the Veil. He passed through the ephemeral barrier into the next world beyond the Dense. He felt the pull within him and he knew immediately where the short journey through the darkness would lead him. Bargavon found himself again at that place. The dead lay before him in heaps of corpses made so by violence, violence handed out by Bargavon himself. He slowly lowered himself to his rock, his contemplative Throne of Death and sat, weariness, sadness and regret weighed heavily upon him. A scraping sound to his left brought his attention to a dark rift between boulders upon the rocky outcropping. From it two black claw-like hands with great effort pulled a dark figure through to a spot several feet away from where he sat. It was the Dark Warrior. It seemed as if it too was tired from great effort. It slowly worked its way up from a crouch to its full height and slowly unsheathed the sword leveling it at Bargavon.

"I realize now our fighting is pointless. Neither of us will win against the other," said Bargavon wearily looking away from the menacing figure and back out to the killing field.

"You could have killed Zhahir easily. Your weakness and empathy have doomed you and continue this agony," hissed the dark one. He stalked closer raising his blade two handed above his head but Bargavon never moved and continued staring out upon the fields. The Dark Warrior was now standing right next to him, the sword ready to drop upon Bargavon's neck. It was if fighting was the only action and the only interaction it fully understood.

"You see all them out there. We did that, together you and me. For what? To further the glory of an Empire? It all seems rather pointless now." Said Bargavon thoughtfully

The Dark Warrior stopped and looked out upon the field of Death; his blade slowly lowered to his side and seemed lost in thought for a moment. "Prince Zhahir would have made a fine addition to it." Whether the Dark Warrior meant it jokingly, Bargavon could not help but laugh for a moment. It all seemed so ridiculous and tragic now.

Neither said anything nor moved for a time, both lost in contemplation at the grotesque carnage. Finally, it was the Dark One that broke the deathly silence, "They deserved it, and I am content in being a vehicle to their demise."

"Some perhaps did deserve to die. We killed some pretty terrible humans who really had it coming. Of those I agree, but to what real end," sighed Bargavon

"The thrill and satisfaction of it, do not deny it. I see beauty in the carnage, the feeling of rage, fear and horror as they died. It filled me with purpose and allowed me expression of death, each a unique death. No two were the same."

"And now? What do you desire now that you are here?" said Bargavon looking up at the dark form standing next to him.

The Dark one said nothing for a moment and then finally with halting words hissed low to barely audible, "I desire for you to remember, to free us of this terribly heavy weight. I have carried it for you for far too long. You think you are strong, but you could not handle what I watch over and protect. Only my hate and violence protect it and only your unwillingness and fear of becoming vulnerable keeps you from facing it. You have made me its guardian for far too long."

"So you, my Dark Warrior are the embodiment of my darkest hate and violence?"

"I protected you from this, tried to show you through what limited perspective I have but no more, you and I have finally come to this now." The Dark Warrior lifted his cloak which drew Bargavon's gaze inward to a field of enveloping darkness. Within, his vision found a patch of pale light that grew into a scene of the young boy holding a crumpled form wrapped in a blanket. The boy Bargavon recognized was himself at age ten. Tears streamed down the boy's olive brown face. He was rocking back and forth sobbing.

Bargavon realized he now stood next to the boy version of himself. He knelt down next to the young Bargavon and saw that there was a small form wrapped within the blanket which the boy held close. He slowly peeled away the cloth, his heart filled with immense dread and emotion welled up within him. A mixture of fear, dread, sorrow, agony, pain, helplessness impaled his soul. The feeling was worse than anything he ever suffered on the battlefield.

In the arms of his younger self was the dead body of his best friend from his youth. It was Dev, the kindest, gentlest soul he had ever met.

"Dev." was all he could eke out from his emotion tightened throat. The name carried with it the memories and feelings of a playful carefree childhood. The flood of sunlit days upon sandy shores, salty water splashing against sun browned bodies and the feel of bare feet climbing up rocks or running down cobblestone streets. It was the sharp peal of laughter and the feeling of stomach butterflies from jumping off high places into turquoise waters. The name carried with it the quiet feeling of just being with someone you tell secrets too and share your dreams. Dev was his first and best friend as a child. They spent their childhood playing all day, carefree along the docks, the sun-splashed streets of the small coastal town of Copra. They talked about going on grand adventures together, sailing the seas, and fighting mythical monsters from the stories they were told.

Childhood, however, ends for boys at age ten when they were required to attend the military academy or in some cases apprenticeship, the priesthood or academia, if they were from wealthy families. It was a quick and brutal end to any childhood. The military academy churned out soldiers and the institution was very good at ripping out the humanness in boys and replacing it with a practical stoicism steeped in fighting, military and imperial doctrine with brutal and efficient applications to serve and expand the Empire.

Early on they trained their bodies and minds for fighting and killing. It was only after three months that they had to pass 'First Kill'. A drill designed to get the conscripts accustomed to killing and death. For 'First Kill' the conscript had to cut the throat of a sheep, goat or rabbit. These animals were raised for wool, hide and eating through the Empire, so killing them in many rural households or a town butcher was a daily occurrence. Bargavon use to watch his uncle back in Copra do it and so with little difficulty performed the task, after all, it might end up being served for dinner that night, if the training group he was in did well on the drills that day.

Dev, however, never had anything close to that experience, quite the opposite. He often found injured small animals and brought them home to nurse them back to health and many times they even lived. Bargavon use to accompany Dev to take these survivors out into the woodlands or coast to let them go. Dev loved animals and his parents even let him keep a few. So kind and empathetic was he, that he was able to domesticate some of his animal patients and keep them as pets. His love of animals was contagious and Bargavon was a willing partner in all Dev's endeavors.

It was Dev's turn upon the killing block. Already he was shaking from what he knew was going to be traumatic. When they placed the knife in his hand, he dropped it and started crying. Bargavon felt his stomach turn. He knew the brutality of the instructors. Nothing good would come of this. There was nothing he could do. If he spoke up for his friend or did anything other than stand at attention, he would be whipped on the pole. They were all made to watch these 'discipline' sessions as it both helped desensitize them to suffering, as well as teach them a lesson to never disobey orders. It took days in the infirmary to heal up and if the healers knew you were in because of a disciplinary action, the treatments were made to be quite callous. The instructors started with slaps to the face and yelling. Again, they forced the blade in his hand, upon which he dropped immediately. His crying only got worse. Next, the switches across his back, then across his face creating thin red welt lines. The hilt of the knife again was thrust into the palm of his hand. The instructor now quite incensed got into Dev's face, "If the knife blade hits the ground again without this animal's blood on it, I will put you will be in the infirmary for a month!"

It was at this time a young boy in exquisite finery was being led by and became interested in the drama that was unfolding. It was of all people the young Prince Zhahir. He was being given a tour led by the school master and with the prince a few attendants. The prince did not have to attend such schooling, but the royals often got complementary tours to oversee the running of their empire. This particular drama appeared to have greatly interested the prince and he suddenly spoke up causing everyone and everything to stop in place. He politely asked what was going on to the school master, who conferred with the instructors a moment. He then returned to tell the prince what was transpiring. The young prince listened, the instructors stood by waiting orders. The young cadets remained at attention, Bargavon barely breathing and Dev stood, tears pouring down his welted face.

Prince Zhahir waved off the instructors and approached Dev. He was about the same age but dressed in gold gilded clothing, jewelry and a jeweled headdress, he was impressive to behold. Dev stood at attention as best he could. Prince Zhahir stepped close. "It seems you do not enjoy killing. I cannot have soldiers like you in my army. If I did, my army would lose, and I cannot have that. I am offering you a chance to redeem yourself and your honor. I command you to kill this goat. If you do not I promise that the instructors will not have to whip you anymore. I will," said the prince with finality in his voice that was unmistakable. He nodded for the instructor to hand Dev the knife.

Dev this time received the knife from the instructor and then did what was quietly talked about by conscripts attending the school for years to come as both an incredulous act and as a warning. Although he couldn't keep the tears from pouring down his face, the shaking stopped in his body and Dev became eerily calm. He looked about and found his friend Bargavon among the silent conscripts standing at attention. Bargavon met his gaze and gave a subtle pleading nod to just kill the animal. Dev smiled sweetly to his friend only a moment and then through blood and tears leveled his gaze up at the towering instructor and then directly at the Prince. His face was covered with tears and welts, but his eyes locked resolutely upon the Prince. He held up the knife and then slowly swept it out to the side for a moment. His palm opened and the knife dropped.

Bargavon could only scream inside, his body fighting the urge to let that scream out. The Prince strode forward snatching a switch from the nearby instructor and down came a barrage of merciless strokes. It lasted perhaps a couple minutes. Dev went down and tried to cover up as best he could. To Bargavon it was an eternity as he could only watch in silent horror as his friend's life was being beaten out of him. The instructors would not interfere and the schoolmaster from behind him politely thanked the Prince for his contribution to the disciplining of the conscript and indicated that he appeared to have had it and would be taken to the infirmary. The Prince seemed incensed the more he beat Dev and in a sudden and surprise act to everyone, retrieved the knife and wrestled the half-conscious Dev up to a sitting position. Prince Zhahir crouched behind him with the knife pressed at his throat.

The school master suddenly stepped forward alarmed, "Prince Zhahir, I applaud your fervor in discipline, but if you would like we can take it from here." Stated the schoolmaster cautiously respectful, but sensing the prince had lost control of his emotions and was trying his best to de-escalate the situation. Bargavon fought against every bodily reflexive contraction to spring across the five yards of ground and knock prince Zhahir onto his ass and save his friend's life. He felt as if he were in a nightmare with no way out.

The knife sliced through the front of Dev's throat, blood gushing forth from the wound and onto the princes' fine gold gilded finery. It was at that moment something shifted in Bargavon, as if his own blood was quickly drained from his body. His insides felt cold, and his arms and legs numbed. His vision collapsed to a narrow field of focus that contained only the Prince killing Dev. Sounds became muffled through his ears except for the clear sound of Prince Zhahir speaking and the gurgle of blood from Dev's throat.

"There, Schoolmaster. I did it. My first kill! That's what you call it right? First Kill." Beamed the blood covered prince dropping Dev's lifeless body onto the ground as if it were one of the sacrificial training animals. Bargavon went numb and remembered nothing of the rest of that week of training. The last thing he saw of Dev before they roughly dragged his lifeless body away was the vacant stare of his face.

Bargavon recognized now that moment back in time. It was at that moment the Empire broke him and made him the callous killing tool he had become. He realized now the Dark Warrior was not created during the mystical experience in the jungle temple. That only allowed him to see it and experience it as separate from him. The Dark Warrior was created at the moment of Dev's death. He was the protective guardian, a deep inner shell that powered his hate while protecting and preserving the memory and love of his friend.

"I am so sorry Dev. There was nothing I could do." Sobbed Bargavon his consciousness melded into his ten-year-old self rocking back and forth holding his dear friend in his arms. Time was not a component beyond the Veil and it could have been a thousand years of such sorrow, but Bargavon slowly returned and found himself crouched upon his Throne of Death overlooking the corpse field. A man of whose entire teenage and adult life was molded into a brainwashed tool of the Medregorian Empire. Clad him in armor, give him the best training for killing and warfare, give him the best weapons and place him in a structure that rewards his sweat and blood for service. In the end it was all just for the greedy whims of a power mad emperor and his equally corrupted sons.

Heaviness and sorrow hung about him upon his throne. His heart ached as it never had in his whole life. Slowly, it started to be paralleled with a searing volcanic hate for Prince Zhahir. It had always been there since the day of Dev's death, but always covered over by the unresolved trauma and effective indoctrination. The hate now was like a low rolling thunder that began to well deep within him, working its way through the strata of his soul. He exploded off the rock and landed on his knees, his scream of rage and hateful vengeance rolled across the dead land like a storm front scattering the carrion birds and bending the twisted trees from its force.

Bargavon sat there upon his knees stunned by the power of his rage from a trauma that he was never truly aware of before. He slowly became aware the Dark Warrior was still there standing quietly by, the deep black form, his red eyes rested upon Bargavon, but their meaning could not be read. There was no solace, no caring, no empathy for the Dark Warrior knew nothing of such concepts. Only hate, malice, rage, vengeance were given to him along with the task of being the wall between Bargavon's childhood, Dev and the cruel outside world.

"Do you see now why Zhahir needs to die. I want to see him burn through every layer of hell and back," said the Dark Warrior though a gravely hiss.

Bargavon slowly stood and faced the Dark Warrior. "I no longer see the way forward. Things are falling apart on the other side in the Dense."

"Vengeance and death are the way forward for us. Now you have a definite purpose back in the Dense. I have given you this." croaked the Dark One, his voice sounded as if spoken like a backwards inhale, speech was not a developed quality in his makeup.

Bargavon shook his head as if filled with cobwebs of doubt, grasping tendrils of despair, and an inner fire of vengeful hate taking root. *Mokantai, where are you? What do I do? Isn't there some remedy for this, some sort of resolution here between the Dark Warrior and myself?*

He turned to see the Dark Warrior striding off across the killing fields. *Why does everyone and everything do this to me here?* He called after "Where are you going?"

The Dark Warrior never looked back but in his mind, he heard him in all his dark rasping blackness "Find Zhahir and kill him to bring him to this side. I will not rest until he is dead. I go to haunt his opium infused dreams. He will not find peace there."

The days aboard the *Sunfire* bound for Kathvitora passed quickly so deep in thought was Bargavon. There was little for the marine detachment to do aboard ship except gamble, tell stories, eat, sleep and watch the beautiful turquoise waters of the Sudarian and then the Arysissar Seas roll past.

His nights found him wandering alone in dark places. His sojourns into the dreamland took him to the dock but the ship was never there. He held the jaguar totem in his hand and called out to Mokantai and even to the Jaguar God for

176

guidance, but no one came until one night he heard barking. He could tell it was Valor and he was grateful for some sort of response. Through the darkness he moved and soon saw his feet were moving across dark earth, moss and tree roots. The air smelled earthy and a night hued jungle soon materialized about him. Through the jungle foliage above a blue-black sky dotted with a million bright stars and a huge crescent moon illuminated silver upon the thick green leaves. Heavy lichen and moss shone silvery green or iridescent lavender upon thick gnarled branches. The moon was setting and beyond a faint purple glow upon the horizon indicated a coming dawn.

Ahead on the trail was Valor wagging his tail, looking back occasionally to see if Bargavon followed. He seemed to have located something or someone. Bargavon had already witnessed Valor's tracking on a few missions with the Company, but this was no Company mission. There was an opening ahead and the sound of crashing water could be heard. He followed the dog up a couple granite boulders that opened to a view of sandy shore sweeping gently outward in an arc. Here the sun had seemed to already be bright and high above. For beyond the Veil in this world, regions existed in the vastness that in and of themselves were whole contained worlds emerging out from the textured blackness of the voids. The sand was white and white gray coral rocks stood out starkly against the incredible blue of the ocean, its waves breaking upon the beach in a frothy end. Upon the coral outcropping stood a boy skipping rocks into the water. Bargavon already knew who it was. It was a scene he had participated in many times in his childhood.

Valor ran ahead and the boy Dev heard his approach, turned and bent to pet him and play with him. Bargavon could see his happy dark almond eyes, his face that radiated pure joy and the hair upon his head so black it nearly looked dark blue in the sun. Bargavon could feel the heaviness begin to drop off him like removing a heavy cloak. He began to pick up his pace, his boots tromped through the rest of the jungle trail that opened to the soft white sand. As he crossed the sand, his pace quickened as he could feel the sun upon his face, his shoulders, his back. He looked down and saw he was no longer in mail, nor burdened with weapons or even the boots he wore moments before. In fact, he was his ten-year-old self, wearing nothing more than a white markip*. He again felt the carefree joy he had once had as he ran to Dev waving his arms overhead like a laughing lunatic. Dev jumped off the outcropping and ran to meet him. They grabbed onto each other jumping, laughing and yelling like exuberant idiots as only boys can do. Valor the dog barked and ran about them, tail wagging, joining in on the fun.

*A markip is a type of loose baggy trousers worn in the regions around the Arysissar Sea. They are made of a light material that dries quickly after getting wet. They are held up by a drawstring around the waist and have similar drawstrings at the ankles. Markips are often tied up at the knees or even over the knees to expose the calves during hot weather or if working around water.

Finally, some sense came to Bargavon. He retained the form of his ten-year-old self, but his mind retained the thirty-year-old warrior veteran consciousness. He had so many things to say, so many questions.

"Dev, I'm....I'm so sorry." He finally got stammered, a sudden solemnness broke out of his joy excitement.

"Barg. I know. It is okay. There was nothing you could have done," replied Dev. A warm smile upon his sun-browned face.

"So much has happened. So much is happening. I don't know where to begin."

"Come Barg, throw some rocks with me, like old times. We can talk for as long as you like," said Dev pulling Bargavon up upon the rocky coral outcropping.

Bargavon felt again all the sensations of his youth, the hot stone upon his feet, its occasional sharpness penetrated his toughened soles. The smell of salt water and the warm sea wind rolled across his sun-bronzed body. He searched along the ground and found many skipping stones that all seemed perfect for throwing. He looked at Dev incredulously at the coincidence.

"This isn't the Dense, Barg." He held out a handful of perfect skippers and laughed.

The two spent the afternoon or whatever timeless moment in the Dev's seaside reality talking and playing. They swam in the warm ocean waters and frolicked with a pod of curious dolphins that came into the cove. Bargavon learned that Dev found purpose helping animals here beyond the Veil, just like he did back in the dense physical world but here he had much greater power and scope. He found like-minded souls that formed a community helping animals. It was his calling and he intended to stay for a while. The dog Valor was the bridge that allowed Bargavon to find the region Dev inhabited. This place they now were in by the seashore was somewhere above and beyond the realms in which Bargavon operated and wandered.

Of Bargavon's condition and situation Dev had only a little insight. He held no ill will toward Zhahir for killing him, in fact, in many ways it elevated him to this beautiful reality and he told Bargavon to let go of the hate he bore for the Prince.

"I cannot see how that is possible. Beyond your world here Dev is a Dark Warrior with whom the pain and trauma binds us. Perhaps together we will resolve it. As to how, I know not. Perhaps I can stay here with you." Inquired Bargavon, for here with his best friend seemed like a heaven.

Dev's face never lost his beautiful smile as he put both hands upon Bargavon's shoulders and looked him deep in his eyes. "Barg, you can come for visits any time, but you have to go back. I may have mastery over my little space here, but I cannot change your path. Know that there is more waiting for you. Just follow Valor to find me. He knows the way now."

"I don't want to go Dev. I am happy here. Now," pleaded Bargavon.

Dev's almond eyes tracked past him and he nodded to someone behind Bargavon. "You have to go Barg. We'll play again I promise."

Bargavon turned and was surprised to see Mokantai the Shaman at the jungle edge, next to him the Jaguar God, its large black body nearly unseen in the dark foliage but its glowing yellow eyes gave it away.

Dev hugged him one last time. Bargavon slumped and trudged back dejected toward the jungle path. Each step seemed heavier and he felt as if a loaded cloak had been draped over him. Darker emotions began to wind their way back through his soul like water percolating through the soil. He looked down, his thirty-year-old legs wore tough baggy pants tucked in heavy leather boots, his torso was clad in chainmail and hanging from a wide leather belt the slap of a sword scabbard at his side and the familiar slap of his ax across a harness upon his back. He looked back one last time to see Dev playing and jumping in the bubbling surf of an incoming wave. He laughed and waved at Bargavon. The dark oppressive mood hung over him once again, but there was a small place in his heart where he captured the joyful energy of Dev, the bright sun and the ocean surf. *I will preserve this memory and keep it with me, no matter how dark my path*. He then wondered if the Dark Warrior had said something similar twenty years ago.

Shaman Mokantai and the Jaguar God met him at the edge of the jungle. He smiled, "Come Medregorian, follow me. I have something to show you. It may give you perspective."

Bargavon said nothing, but followed. He was sad to leave the happiness of his best friend and was not looking forward to what awaited him upon his return to the physical world. They traversed the path through the jungle and back into the nighttime world of the crescent moon and bright stars above the dark jungle canopy. They traveled up to a higher elevation and ended up upon a mountain that broke free of the jungle. Here he could see in all directions of the night sky around him.

The stars seem to get brighter. The space between them blacker and the land about them began to blur. He stood next to Mokantai and looked out upon the majesty of the universe spread before him. To his right the large black cat known as the Jaguar God sat next to him, so large was he that even sitting his eyes were level with Bargavon standing. Mystery and power emanated from the feline god.

Mokantai finally spoke while continuing to gaze out at the beauty before them. "Medregorian, you have seen the dark pockets, the black pits and the deep troughs in the Universe and you have done great service to both yourself and others by helping them up to higher ground, to where they once again can progress ever onward on their paths. That is the way of things, for all things, always in motion, evolving, expanding. Sometimes we lose the way for a while or need to remain in place for a time to learn, to integrate, and to understand before we are allowed to go onward."

"I have mostly seen darkness, pain, war, cruelty. Even on this side, my existence encompasses essentially the same. If it wasn't for seeing Dev just now or Krin back in the Dense I would have little moments of joy and happiness left in my life at all." replied Bargavon contemplating the Shaman's words.

"Cherish those moments you just spoke of in the Dense, for they are worth all the pain you go through. Life is short in the Dense, appreciate what time you are given, especially with that which brings you joy. All things come to an end and a new cycle begins. Eternity is what you have on this side. Despite your nightly sojourns blindly stumbling through the void or violence filled missions with the Company, you have only seen the smallest of slivers here beyond the Veil. Come, you should at least be shown a small tour for it may give you solace and hope when all seems darkest." With that Mokantai blew out a stream of pipe smoke that slowly took the faintly shimmering shape of an arched bridge that seem to reach out into the star-filled sky. He then directed Bargavon's attention to the Jaguar God with his pipe.

"You can only come with us on this journey, if you ride on the back of the Jaguar God," said Mokantai tapping out the ash from his pipe and securing it in his pouch. Bargavon climbed aboard the great cat carefully for he had much respect for the creature that once crushed his nonphysical essence in its jaws.

They stepped off the cliff and onto the faint tracing of the bridge of smoke that arched upward into the vast heavens. He rode astride the great cat and felt its powerful body moving gracefully beneath him. Next to him walked Mokantai, his dark face covered with tattoos was serene. As they walked, the stars seemed to get brighter and it was if they passed by these stars, nebula and other celestial objects Bargavon could not describe. Distance and time were irrelevant. Bargavon's vision began to see overlays of scenes and scenery as if they were great windows or portals into strange and indescribable realms. Some of these they entered and passed through. Places that seemed just like his world, but with races he had never seen before. Environments most earthlike, but of such shimmering beauty that anything he had seen in the Dense was a pale copy.

They passed by god-like beings or titans playfully casting bolts of lightning from towering mountain peaks to each other and then back again. They saw the Medregorian god Kasemus along with other gods of luck and chance from other pantheons at a great table gambling with the lives of their corporal followers. The table reminded Bargavon of the Yendessi boards but on a vastly more complex scale.

They passed by a neutron star. Its x-rays bathing as it blasted system radioactive death. Nothing should live there in the Dense, but here beyond the Veil, some mysterious intelligence had built great obelisks of solid tungsten metal.

The large structures tumbled slowly in space far out from the dead star, their purpose unknown.

Moving beyond these celestial vistas, they entered a region of an endless perfect summer day. Above was a bright blue sky with just a few clouds, the temperature warm and comfortable with a faint breeze. People were here relaxing, talking, playing and the joy emanated from every rock, tree, blade of grass or shimmering ripple of water.

From the summer like region they passed into a realm of a perpetual sunset. They soared above a layer of clouds, majestic in their structure, each a great mountain or billowing citadel in the sky. The sunset far off cast rays that imbued the clouds with yellows, pinks, purples, orange and gold. Ever changing were the colors and the cloud structures.

On and on they continued through landscapes and regions each uniquely spectacular until they passed through a silvery white shimmering field of cool light of the moon and they were once again upon a great arch of a bridge that dropped down out of a starry sky and back upon the jungle mountaintop where they had started their journey.

Bargavon slid off the back of the Jaguar God and stood looking up into the night sky. His senses slowly taking in the surroundings; the sound of the waterfall, the chirp of crickets, the earthy smell of the jungle soil and rich green moss, the feel of the zephyr of cool moisture upon his face, churned up from the waterfall in the gorge below. Bargavon took in a deep breath and wondered if it was his first breath since starting the grand tour.

He finally spoke, "There is so much out there."

"There is and so much more," replied Mokantai crushing another dried leaf in his pipe. "The Jaguar God took you on a quick tour of just some of the places we have roamed. The inquisitive soul always seeks to reach the far horizon and see what is beyond."

"And, what have you discovered Shaman?" questioned Bargavon, his mind trying hard to make logical connections with all the places they had seen.

The Shaman's pipe seemed to magically light by the deft wave of Mokantai's hand. "More vistas and horizons, ever onward."

Chapter 10

Endings and Vengence

The *Sunfire* pulled into port and the troops disembarked. Bargavon played his roll well as a non-descript marine to not draw any extra attention his way. At an opportune moment, he ditched his marine attire and blended into the busy streets of Kathvitora, making haste to his house. He needed to get Krin and his father out of the city and to safety along with whatever he could carry. The *Sunfire* should have taken a direct route to the capitol, but was instead held up at Vizercenza for four days due to minor hull damage suffered in the battle. Quick repairs were performed but not quick enough for Bargavon and it took all he had to remain a marine bored with guard duty while his swirling thoughts dug a well-worn rut of anxiety fueled footprints in his brain. If word got to Kathvitora ahead of him, the Prince may have sent men to his home to wait for him. Bargavon was extra cautious and expected the worse. Targ may have done his best to create a story of his death including probably dressing up a crushed body in his armor and personal effects but the Royals were a conniving lot and they were experts at intrigue and lies. Zhahir may not be so easily fooled.

Moving up the street he turned down an alley. This alley was essentially a small street and was populated by many small businesses and small taverns. He ducked into one called The Blue Sphinx's Goblet. The sign out front showed a blue colored sphinx lounging on its side downing a frothy mug. A partially opened heavy curtain served as the door to this small establishment. Bargavon moved down the two steps off the street into the smoky dark interior. It was a cramped place and the ceiling was low at perhaps seven feet high. Only four men were here talking over their pints of ale or wine. A few oil lamps cast a low light and the place smelled of sour wine juxtaposed with the sweet spicy smell of the proprietor's pipe smoke. Janus the tavern keeper saw Bargavon and gave a slight nod. His face went from standard workday boredom to slightly worried. He knew that if Bargavon were here, there was personal trouble.

Years ago, Bargavon rescued this tavern-keeper who was traveling back from the Northern Marches in a small caravan. The caravan fell under attack by a Northman raiding party and Bargavon's company was going north at that moment toward Kuska near the northern border. It was fortunate timing. The Medregorians drove off the raiders and Bargavon personally saved Janus from being hacked to pieces under Northman powered axes. Janus was grateful and offered whatever he had for his life. Bargavon refused but finding out Janus had a tavern in Kathvitora said that maybe he would stop in for a pint every now and then. This he did about once a year but there was one thing he asked the tavern keeper to do for him. It was really just a small favor. Bargavon kept an emergency cache in a back room in the tavern.

Janus looked about and saw the only four customers were half drunk and just had new mugs placed before them. He nodded for Bargavon to follow him past another curtain hung in a doorway opposite the street entrance. This room was even darker, lit by another oil lamp on a shelf that Janus turned up to cast more light. Here were wooden casks of ale and wine, along with a dozen bottles of other spirits, a small washbasin with water that should have been emptied a while ago, some towels hanging on hooks and a shelf of a variety of mugs, goblets and a few larger tankards. Beyond this a small hallway to a few rooms that were his personal quarters.

"Looks like you should empty your wash basin. The water is a little grayish," stated Bargavon breaking the silence.

"Shhhh Captain, that's where I wash the mugs and my hands. It flavors the drinks. Proprietary secret," smiled Janus through his bushy mustache.

"Your ale and wine might taste better if what they were served in was a little cleaner," replied Bargavon picking up a mug off the shelf to sniff at it.

"Are you out of your mind! The wine I serve is so sour and the ale is so bitter I need that 'extra something' to make it palatable. Remember this tavern is on Rev's Alley not Jade Street." Responded Janus taking the mug from Bargavon, rolling his eyes and placing it back on the shelf. "Come on, the chest is back here in my room, I sense you are in a bit of a hurry."

Bargavon followed him back to a small but tidy bedroom. Janus carried the oil lamp back to give light to the room. "I kept it under my bed for safekeeping." grunted Janus pulling a heavy wooden chest out from under the bed. Bargavon opened the lid. Inside a chainmail shirt, a weapon belt with a dagger in a scabbard, a longsword in a scabbard, a leather belt with pouches, most of these holding gold, silver and copper coins, one held a handful of small gems that he had pried off items from conquests over the years. A new set of plain traveling clothes, sandals, cloak, a wineskin and some forged documents he had scribed up that might get him out of trouble. He changed his clothes and donned the mail shirt, belt, weapons belt and changed his sandals all in quick order. The tavern keeper had left him be and went to attend to his customers. Bargavon helped himself to a steel goblet of ale and quickly washed it down. *It really is that bad,* he thought pouring himself another from the tap.

Bargavon found Janus's back door and exited into a narrow alley that wound its way out to one of the main streets that would lead to his house. He strode quickly through the crowd although he felt a growing sense of urgency. He would run if he could but did not want to attract attention. It was only minutes but seemed much longer when he arrived at his home and already sensed his worst fears had come true. Three men were outside the home, they looked like paid thugs. Big men dressed in armor or studded leather shirts. Heavy clubs, swords and daggers were obvious upon their person. A fourth staggered out into the streets, blood was pouring from a slash across his abdomen and his hands were not doing an adequate job holding it back. The other three were startled and ran to him as he collapsed.

"Who would have thought he kept a she-wolf in his home. Katoblir and Jhop lie within dead. Caprian might be alive but his breaths were coming shallow. I ran her through. She is as good as dead. So is the old man."

"Vicus, get him away and call for a few more men. We need to clean this up and await his return. We will take him unawares within.

Bargavon's heart was pounding in his throat, the blood began to boil in his veins. The sword began to slide out its scabbard, the pommel grasped tightly in an iron grip. *It's over and I am too late my Krin. My father, I am so sorry. At least, I will avenge you.*

"I am already here," stated Bargavon in a low menacing growl. His mailed frame stalked out from the shadows, sword drawn. Waves of revenge and hate wafted off him and his eyes burned of hungry death. He moved to the grouping of men with a sole purpose of death and ruin. The three men quickly drew weapons and dropped back, the forth simply slumped weakly to the cobblestone with a grunt. Bargavon strode forward with measured confidence and he came upon the man holding his stomach wound upon the cobblestone, lopped his head off as if casually parting a branch. *They know who they face. Bargavon, Hero of the Empire, but most immediately a vengeful husband and son. They know they are doomed. I can feel their fear.*

The first man came at him with a wild series of poorly aimed blows which Bargavon easily parried away. Now Bargavon swung down hard and the man's sword came up in a weak parry which was blown back by a powerful sword stroke and quickly circled past with a chop through his face. The next attacker moved up to his left flank but Bargavon ducked low into a squat and sprung upward driving his head under the jaw of this man with a loud crack, breaking his jaw knocking him out.

That left just one attacker to deal with who had tried to circle around him during his combat while he was occupied with the other two. Bargavon wheeled to parry a downward blow by the man's club and twisted his sword back to drive a thrust into his opponent's torso. Impaling him on the sword he lifted him up two hands upon the hilt of the impaling sword and flung him several feet away where he landed writhing in severe pain, his guts were strewn a few feet out from him. His eyes bulged trying to reconcile his life's end.

He returned to the second man with the broken jaw. He was slowly coming too and moaning. His eyes opened to see the dark form of Bargavon standing above him driving his longsword straight down into his chest.

Bargavon made his way into the house, sword drawn and his senses heightened. Shallow gasping breaths led him to a hallway where a thug lay upright against the way, half his left arm and flank had been gashed open and blood pooled about him. His head slowly turned toward Bargavon's approach, his face was white and pale. "You must be Caprian." Bargavon walked past him and casually slit his throat as if an afterthought.

The hallway opened up into the great room. It was in disarray from recent combat. Two more thugs lay dead, sword strokes were apparent on arms, legs, torso and heads. *Krin had made a good account for her Northern heritage. She was so strong, so brave and defiant, my beautiful Krin.*

There upon a great chair sat Krin. She was leaning half forward onto the Fybsuvian bastard sword, its blade deep red from blood. She herself was in her ivory gown, now mostly red soaking up her own copious amounts of blood. She looked as if she had died in that position, the sword being the only thing propping her upright. Her eyes were locked across the room at the man who's throat Bargavon slit.

Bargavon knelt before her, emotion welling up within him. He choked back tears ineffectually as he reached out to touch her but stopped short as if she were a fragile bubble and any touch would finally break her form. "Krin, I am so sorry I was not here to protect you." He whispered through clenched teeth and tears. The vulnerability he so feared had been exploited and he was at its mercy.

"What did you bring me?" Came her reply in the weakest of whispered breath

Bargavon carefully removed the Fybsuvian sword from her clenched grasp. He sat on the great chair and pulled her onto his lap. Her body was limp and pale from loss of blood. He embraced her close and whispered softly in her ear, his tears fell upon her cheeks. He pulled forth the gold and diamond ring he had taken in Wuxano and to show her. "My beautiful Krin, I have brought you this ring to ask you to be my wife, but I am afraid I have also brought your death."

Krin weakly lifted her head from his shoulder and looked at him "Thank you, my Captain, my Love, I accept both your gifts." And at that she kissed him one last time as life finally left her body. He held her there pressed against him for some time, not caring if more assassins would come. Eventually, he laid her form down gently and searched the home finding his father dead near his beloved Yendessi boards, the pieces blood-spattered and strewn across the courtyard.

An hour later found Bargavon high upon a rocky hill overlooking the city. He risked the fact that he was not a known outlaw yet and Prince Zhahir was keeping his vengeance quite private. The slandering and demonizing of Bargavon publically would happen soon by royal decree. To the average soldiers and watchmen, he was still Captain Bargavon, hero of the Empire at least for a short time more. He had wrapped Krin in a cloak and placed her over a horse. He led her out the Northgate after making small talk with the sentries who knew him. He headed up out of the city.

He knew his time was short as he built a makeshift funeral pyre out of the many rocks that lined the hill as well and dry kindling he found nearby. He knew enough of the Northern ways that warriors and chieftains were burned in boats set adrift on the sea or upon funeral pyres upon the mountain sides. She was fierce and of a warrior's heart, so he would do this to honor her.

He carried her over to the pyre. He lowered her down gently upon the kindling, placed the ring upon her finger and smoothed out her hair. "There were few in life I ever trusted and very few that I ever kept close to my heart. It seems all my adult life my name has been bathed in glory for the Empire and blood of all who opposed it. All I ever seem to do is bring death and ruin even upon the one I loved. My glory and all my victories are hollow compared to the time I shared with you. Goodbye, my beautiful Krin. Maybe we will meet again beyond the Veil."

He bent down and kissed her lips, then placed a burning brand upon the byre. The kindling lit and soon fire engulfed the body that was once Krin. Bargavon stood back and watched. The firelight glinted off his wet eyes and his coat of mail. He knew they were coming for him and he was not going to leave this place. Here is where he would die, by the ashes of his love. And so he spent the late hours of the night, unmoving before the funeral pyre. Glowing embers wafted up into the starry night and the only sound was a gentle wind and the crackle of the fire.

At dawn they had found him. Behind him came the sound of horse hooves upon turf and rocky ground and the clink of armor. Bargavon turned from the now low burning funeral pyre. He was surrounded by close to forty men on horseback. By the looks of their arms and armor they were Royal House Guards, but Bargavon expected this. He drew his sword. He would die here next to the burning body of Krin. It was as good of an end as any.

"Captain Bargavon, put down your sword. We did not come here to kill you. You are being summoned to meet with Prince Zhahir. Apparently, there was some misunderstanding that happened in Wuxano and he just wanted to clear everything up so that no false rumors or stories are spread."

"And by 'summoned' you mean taken prisoner and led to the dungeons. I am mourning the loss of my companion and I am not in the summoning mood. Commander, I am afraid you did not bring enough men for me to kill tonight. Please send one of your riders back into the city for more, preferably Prince Zhahir if he has arrived. My sword is quite thirsty for his blood."

"I'm afraid I cannot do that, Captain, as his Highness is still on the way from Wuxano. He did want to see you personally."

"I am tired of talking. Killing is more to my liking right now." As Bargavon strode confidently forward his sword raised to cleave the Royal Guard Commander, a dart punctured his neck. *Poison! The cowards.* The world went black.

Chapter 11

Prison & Pain

The days and nights became one long nightmare. What little unconsciousness he was allowed did not afford him the relief to pass through the Veil. He would see it and reach out, but was always wakened at the last minute to the thrust back into pain and misery of the Dense. When he returned to the Dense he was never sure he was there for many times he saw things that belonged on the other side present in the physical. His worlds were blending. He had no track of days or nights. He was in a pitch-black cell that smelled of unmistakable smell of shit and the sour smell of vomit and piss. He was frequently beaten, whipped and tortured in several imaginative ways. In between, he was given food and water that was barely passable for animal consumption and possibly poisoned to make him sicker. Delirious nightmares, unrelenting vertigo and nausea would then wash over him until the next round of torture.

Perhaps the torturer had the night off, but Bargavon made it passed the Veil and for a few moments enjoyed the feeling of no pain of his physical body. His heart however was another matter. The thought of the loss of Krin and his father was overwhelming and for the first time since the night of his capture he had a moment to grieve. Emotion here beyond the Veil was a holistic sensation. It seemed every fiber, every particle every thought vibrated with the grief and sadness. All-encompassing was its effect and he closed in on himself, his perception of the textured blackness faded into heavy dark grey waves of sorrow.

He felt a sudden blinding flash of pain that brought him back to the Dense immediately. Had he been gone a few seconds, minutes, hours? There was no further contemplation of this as fists rained down upon his face and head. "Time to wake up traitor!" bellowed his torturer. Another round of brutality was to begin.

At some point while on a rack being tortured, he started passing out from the pain and it was then he saw Cobra standing right behind one of the torturers looking on disapprovingly and shaking her head in disgust. He could hear a man faintly "He's done. Drag him back to the cell for a few hours."

He was vaguely aware of being lifted and then roughly dumped onto the cool stone floor of his cell. When the jailors left all was black again. He thought his eyes were closed but maybe they were open. He could faintly make out the cell and a form standing in the cell. It reached down and dragged him some distance that made no sense as it was farther than the cell was wide until he recognized the Veil that he passed through.

Bargavon stood up, feeling completely well and in normal condition for this side of the Veil. Before him stood Cobra and next to him the dog Valor.

Before he could speak Cobra interrupted him "I got tired of waiting, so I crossed over to find you. I see you were spending some time playing children's games with the other humans."

Bargavon looked back to the Veil, grateful for the physical and mental respite from the torture even if it meant fighting horrible things in dark and dreary places. "I wouldn't call it play. I am in a bad spot. I'm being tortured in a prison pretty much round the clock."

"Tortured!" blurted Cobra is disbelief "What a bunch of rank amateurs. I would hardly call that torture. I could show them a few things that would really be far more effective."

"You're a fucking asshole, Cobra. Born in Hell gives you inherent professional credentials in matters of pain and torture, so I am going to forget you think that I am playing back there. I am nearly dead I think. Better I die so I can be here full time. I am beginning to like it better here now that my father and my love have passed beyond the Dense and are hopefully in some sort of blissful state here."

"How quaint and very human of you, Medregorian, we shall pick flowers for your sweetie on the way." Replied Cobra her voice dripping with sarcasm. Valor barked and wagged his tail. Cobra looked down at the dog. "He's been by your side the whole time back there."

Bargavon looked up "How do you know? Have you come to visit often?"

"Yes, I have. I whisper helpful techniques in the torturer's ear, but he never seems to execute them well. Actually, I'm beginning to miss you. Your brutally effective skill at killing demons, devils, abyssal denizens and spectral ghouls are kind of a turn on for me. This business here being tortured as you call it is keeping you out of some of the runs. The Commander said to find you and get you back to the ship for the next run.

"Is that true?" spoke Bargavon intrigued.

"About the upcoming run? Yes. Also, yes about the torturer too. What a lummox. If I were there in the Dense, I would have you screaming in several octaves relegated only to the females of your species and I would pull all your guts out and then make you put them all back in again."

Bargavon listened for a few more moments as Cobra happily described several more horrible acts unique to the torments of Hell. Bargavon finally held up a hand. "That is all very nice Cobra, but let me remind you all those wonderful sounding procedures would immediately result in death in the Dense and so perhaps limit the duration of your play time."

Cobra seemed perplexed at the notion. Bargavon finally pointed forward into the gloom. Chant was there standing at the entrance to a bridge that exited from the edge of the darkened gloom. "Are you two done having sex or whatever your kind do. The rest of the company is waiting. We got another run to do"

Bargavon looked at Cobra askance "Sex?"

Cobra ignored the question and strode quickly before him, "Come on, we're going to be late." She sneered and flashed her fangs at the massive baboon like Chant as she passed him.

Bargavon reached Chant as he followed and raised an inquisitive eyebrow. "There's a wager on you and Cobra going on in the Squad," said Chant in a soft voice.

'Wager on what?" inquired Bargavon leaning into Chant momentarily taking his eyes off Cobra strutting before him in the gloom. Chant's silver markings rippled and brightened and as he bent down to speak his eyes snapped open in sudden surprise and he stood up rigidly.

"I should probably just lead you back to the ship." Chant said awkwardly. For a second Bargavon was baffled until he moved away and saw that Cobra had been behind the big warrior with a long black curved dagger she had moments ago pressed into Chant. Her ability to change her location was one of her natural and very useful traits. She smiled presenting her small fangs, her yellow snake-like eyes held a touch of mischievousness. Bargavon didn't press further. He knew he was not going to crack the mystery with Cobra.

The Company had secured its retrievals from the maze like catacombs here in the Abyssal plane. Bargavon was part of the rear guard detachment as the rest of the company made its way back to the ship. It was the first run Bargavon had since being taken prisoner and tortured. He assumed the length of time that allowed him this run with the company was due to a day off of the torturer or perhaps they were leaving him alone to die. If it wasn't for the deep grief he felt for Krin, he would have enjoyed this violent and gore filled vacation here in the Abyss. Perhaps there is a way out of all of this. I am just so tired of the endless struggle, thought Bargavon.

He saw the group of locust like guardians lunge forward into their line. He threw himself with fury into their masses flailing berserker like with both ax and sword. Their blades wrecking ruin upon the beasts. He was a man possessed. They struck at him with their sharp talons and saw-like appendages gashing him terribly. Bargavon bled from several wounds, his mail crimson with his own blood. He felt his body going numb. A guardian ran him through with a claw. Its end pierced out his back. Bargavon hissed and gasped at the shocking blow. The warrior within him kept driving rage and violence into his body, his sword skewered his attacker and his ax beheaded it even as it held him in his claw. Down they went but Bargavon staggered back up laughing. *Perhaps this was the desperate but comical feeling Big Red had as I slew him.* Blood gushed from his chest as he threw himself forward killing two more with wild swings, but in the process he was put down as a slashing talon that ripped away most of his right leg. His world started to blur as his vision only caught flashing shapes and light. *I am going to die here in the world beyond the Dense, just as I will soon die in the physical world, I have done all I can and I don't want any more.* The world around him faded to black.

He awoke to indescribable pain. Lancing and searing from several areas of his body, it was a strange combination of crushing numbness and stabbing fire. Above him the pleasant face of Smiling Gold whose hands seemed to be everywhere at once pressing here, pulling on something in a different location, pulling tubing filled with glowing light and pressing it into couplings of metallic looking tools and apparatuses that were attached to Bargavon. Blood suddenly sprayed across Smiling Gold's faceplate, Bargavon realized it was from him. He couldn't move, he seemed to be strapped down. Bargavon had vision only out of one eye, but he saw some of his comrades huddled nearby. Gage and Big Red were trying to muscle past to see him. Their faces looked grim and he detected even a bit of worry. A medic tried to shoo them off and then got angry with them for getting in the way. They reluctantly departed but just behind them sat Big Blue on a bench watching with him concerned interest.

Bargavon heard someone screaming nearby, most likely another warrior pulled from the battle being worked on by the medics. He realized a second later it was coming from him. He must have been torn apart real bad for he noted at least three medics on him, all working feverishly and all covered in a lot of blood, his blood.

A medic was shoved away from him and Cobra stepped into view of his good eye. Her beautifully fiendish face was pulled back taut in both concern and anger "Medregorian, you are not getting out of this easily. What did you think would happen? That you would just die on this side and it would all go away?" She looked up at Smiling Gold, her snake eyes narrowed intensely "He'll make it right?"

"I'm trying Cobra my dear but there was a fragment of him previously missing and it would have been a little easier if it were still here. I am a class 'A' Astral Medic, not a miracle worker. He's a broken wreck as he is... It's as if there is not enough of him left to pull together. We might lose him"

"Trans-Essence me!" commanded Cobra

Smiling Gold stopped his work abruptly at looked into Cobra's desperate face. Big Blue stood up with a start. Everyone halted their work and all seemed frozen in time except the sound of screaming that Bargavon heard as himself, as if he were disembodied from his own vocal chords. Smiling Gold shot a glance at Big Blue.

"It's her call. I will authorize it," said Big Blue solemnly

"This is really going to hurt Cobra and you're going to take a long while to mend up from this. It is not like battle wounds," explained Smiling Gold, returning to his work, his blood and gore covered hands reaching toward his assistant for another tool. The other medics returned to a flurry of activity, the feeling of some sort of soothing white light was starting to now be faintly palpable at the far edges of the deep sea of Bargavon's pain.

Cobra blinked her yellow reptilian eyes for a moment, letting the weight of her decision settle upon her. She looked to Big Blue.

"Your call Cobra, I support it whatever way you choose," spoke Big Blue gravely

Cobra looked down at Bargavon. "Human, you going to fucking owe me." She looked back to Smiling Gold. "Ok, let's do this."

Bargavon's world warped again into delirious waves of incredible pain, interspersed by probing fingers of soothing healing light that continued to slowly break down the pain's all-encompassing hold upon him. Fragments of chopped memory flashed across his consciousness; his screams, the pictures of Smiling Gold and the other medics, crunching and thumping sounds, a view of the Commander standing by him, the far off screaming of someone else joining his own in a chorus. *Was it Cobra? What did she subject herself to save me and why?* These thoughts barely made it through his delirium and the screaming was getting louder.

Quickly, the far off screaming rose to a raw guttural roar. There was a blinding flash of light and the crack of the bullwhip lanced fire across his back. Bargavon was back in the Dense, back in his tortured physical body, pain throbbed and stabbed from everywhere but oddly less so than what he awoke from. Somewhere deep within him he had to laugh at the other ridiculousness of the situation. *Pain and torture in two worlds simultaneously, I must have some skill to pull this off.*

"Enough!" bellowed a gruff voice. "Anymore and will kill him. The Prince will put us to the block if we push it too far. Drag him back to the cell." As he was dumped roughly on the filth covered floor we felt fingers jam something into the crook of his arm.

A day passed or so Bargavon thought for he sat in darkness. For once the usual torture came to a stop and there were no beatings today. He ran his fingers over the small object someone had placed in the crook of his arm the previous day. Even in the darkness he knew what it was for he was familiar with every curve and edge of the stone jaguar totem. He wondered who gave him this small gesture of humanity and why, but he was grateful.

His food still consisted of mostly rotten scraps and filthy water. At least, that was what it looked like in the brief exposure of torchlight carried by the jailor, as he slid the wooden bowls through the slot in the bars. He spent the better part of his time in the darkness thinking about what had befallen Cobra and his own body beyond the Veil. His thinking was broken up occasionally by the feel of whiskers, the claw of a rat or the occasional nibble to see if he was carrion. Despite his weakened state, he could still swipe at his invisible attackers in the dark; occasionally connecting his fist or kick of a foot with a furry body that he heard a squeak and scamper away. He managed to grab one and crush it with his hands. He tossed away the dead rodent to some unseen part of his cell. He thought of eating it for more nourishment, but decided it would divert the other rats from him for a while as they fed on a truly dead carcass. At some point, sleep overtook him and it was a dark dreamless sleep. No Veil, no contact from beyond. There was nothing but unconsciousness.

The next day, he awoke to torchlight. A largish hooded jailor was placing it in a wall sconce. He said nothing as he turned and stared at Bargavon within the cell, his face hidden in the cowl of the hood. He remained silent. Bargavon's entire body was agony, but he found he could almost stand despite weakness and severe injuries. For the first time, he could see his surroundings. A stone cell blackened with centuries of human misery. Filth, burns, caked blood and bruises blackened his body. Outside the iron bars of his cell the low-lit torch showed a larger chamber with walls set with manacles, empty of inhabitants and old bones lay beneath them, perhaps past occupants. A dark narrow hallway led off.

There was a far off sound of metal jangling, the mechanism of a lock and the creak of a rusty hinge. Another light came from down the hallway and the sound of several boots echoed. Soon several men strode across the larger chamber to his cell. Most were jailers, large ugly men in leather or quilted jerkins armed with clubs, a royal guardsman in silvered mail and another man hooded man well dressed in a fine cloak. In the torchlight that was now behind this figure, he stopped for a moment to inspect Bargavon behind the bars. He began to speak and immediately his identity became known to him.

"How do you like your new accommodations Bargavon, Disgraced Hero of the Empire? The atrocities I have heard that you committed in Wuxano were shameful," said Zhahir mockingly. "You are now my guest here in the dungeons below the grand palace. This particular cell hasn't been used in a few generations I think. It was reserved for those the family wished to just forget about and let rot. You have provided great amusement for me over the last several weeks. I have really enjoyed our time together."

Several weeks then, right, thought Bargavon to himself, finally getting a clear understanding of the time.

Prince Zhahir pulled back the hood exposing his perfumed oiled locks to the torchlight. His face smelled of rosewater and his clothes of exotic sweetness. Bargavon stared at him from his one partially opened eye. The other seemed not to open. *Might be swollen shut or maybe I'm blind there now. Prince Zhahir, I will live and I will kill you, and if I don't I know a certain someone on the other side who I am quite sure will deliver the vengeance for us both.*

"Believe it or not, I actually got tired of beating and torturing you. You see, there was always so much blood and filth with our get-togethers I would have to spend the rest of the night in the baths soaking it all away. That…became a bother."

Bargavon tried to verbalize a retort, but his mouth felt numb and his throat so dry and painful from hurling out screams of pain he managed only a croak and groan. The prince only smiled with disdain.

"I saw through General Targ's feeble attempt at protecting you. I am going to give him a temporary pass on his transgression. I have heard something of you military types and your 'warrior codes', blah, blah, blah. I am going to make sure I send him off on some fool's excursion to put an end to his otherwise exemplary military career. But that is later and now he serves me well as Army General in my new Principality of Wuxano. Oh, and as for your loyal men that were under your command, I am afraid to be the bearer of bad news, but it appears their ships left Wuxano and a few days later the wreckage washed back up on shore. Something terrible must have happened." Spoke the prince feigning a concern. "No survivors I'm afraid." The prince let that sink in for a moment.

Prince Zhahir leaned in close to the bars, his voice barely above a whisper "I could not have you going around spreading stories about what you thought you saw in Wuxano. Untrue as they are, Eh Bargavon? Heroes die Bargavon. The most glorious ones die a heroic death in battle serving a noble cause, but not you. You were thrown in prison for your cowardice and atrocities you committed in Wuxano. At least, that is what I am having the battle records drawn up say. That will be your legacy," smiled the prince, his white teeth gleaming in the torchlight.

"I'll see you in Hell," croaked out Bargavon giving a weak bloody smile.

"Quite unlikely, my lineage is tied to the gods. I am literally guaranteed a place at the divine feast of the Ninety-Nine."

Bargavon managed a weak chuckle, and then coughed out flecks of blood through a wheezing laugh that ended in a series of coughs and groans

"You're going to die here." The prince stood up and turned to his men. He gave the last orders to the hooded jailor who stood silently by the torch. "Starve him slowly and let him rot here. I am returning to my new palace at Wuxano. Send me word when he is dead." He turned and strode back down the passage.

The next day, he was awoken by the sound of his food bowl being slid under the narrow opening of the bars of his cell. A lone torch placed in a bracket gave off a smoky light. It was the hooded jailor from the previous day.

"The prince said to starve you to death slowly. He didn't say how slowly," chuckled the jailor.

Perplexed, Bargavon reached for his bowl and in the dim torchlight saw there was a wooden spoon in it. The bowl was full to the brim and if he wasn't hallucinating, the smell and sight looked of beef stew. A wooden mug held clear cool water. *I guess I have truly snapped. This actually looks and smells like real food.* He decided to enjoy the olfactory and sensory mirage while it lasted and ravenously ate and drank. He never got a chance to use the spoon. It truly was the best food he could recall eating. *Probably poisoned though, I'll be throwing up soon.* He finished and only then realized the jailor was still there, a monstrous form holding up the torch. The jailor had pulled back his hood revealing his face flickering in the yellow light and Bargavon could see a smile upon his face.

"I know you," said Bargavon, his voice but a strained whisper.

"Yes Captain, it's me, Vasardev," said the hulking jailor "I couldn't do anything while the Prince was here, but he's gone. It really was hard to see you go through it all, Sir, but help is on the way. Just stay strong a little longer."

"It was you who gave me back my jaguar totem."

"Yes Sir, and I was able to keep out the poison they were dumping in your food on most days. There was not much else I had control over," said Vasardev.

Bargavon reached his fingers through the bars and clasped Vasardev's hand in thanks. He then nodded and then slow trudged away down the corridor leaving Bargavon in the now familiar darkness of his prison, but now with the feeling of hope.

Chapter 12

The Redemption Run

Bargavon had a quiet night in his cell. His strength returned a little with the nourishment although he was riddled with injuries both minor as well as severe. His success this night at killing a couple rats with his bare hands afforded him an undisturbed length of sleep.

He appeared before the Veil and passed through half expecting the pain and horror that he left his body in. He entered the textured black void and he felt normal. There was no pain or injury. He looked down. All his arms and legs seemed whole. His armor of fine chainmail was upon him. His sword, dagger and ax were in their normal places. All evidence of terrible wounds was absent. He had seen wounds heal far quicker than normal upon the warriors by the medics' skills after battles but not to the extent he had suffered. Next to him padding about was Valor, wagging his tail licking Bargavon's hand. He reached down and petted Valor. "What a good boy you are Valor. I have no idea what awaits me anymore on either side of the Veil.

A magnetic pull within him soon led him and Valor to the dock. The ramp into the ship had just been lowered and out strode Gage and Big Red.

"Hey Fucker, are you ready to get back to work or are you still on vacation?" boomed Big Red, his face showed a glower that was more for show than real.

"I guess. I have had some difficulties as of late," replied Bargavon striding up the ramp. Gage said nothing but smiled warmly and shook his hand.

Bargavon suddenly stopped cold on the ramp. The other two warriors took note, stopped and turned back. "What is it, getting cold feet for this great fun we get to have?" chided Big Red.

"No, I just wondered what happened to me after I left, and to Cobra. I think she did something for me that I do not understand but seemed to be at great personal cost. Because of it I am here whole and sound."

The two warriors looked at each other for a moment. Finally, Gage smiled and slapped Bargavon on his mailed shoulder, "Come on, everything is okay. Smiling Gold can debrief you inside."

They entered the ship and all seemed normal; warriors busking for combat, donning armor and adjusting equipment, loading weapons and cracking jokes or just grumbling to themselves. A few saw him and acknowledged him with a nod. He made his way to Big Blue and the squad. Here they were all smiles. Lots of jovial physical contact, warm hellos as they welcomed him back. His eyes sought out Cobra. She stood up and smiled cautiously. She approached slowly and the others stepped away. Bargavon just stood. He was happy she appeared to be okay and whole. When she got face to face with him she clasped his head with her powerful hands and drew him to her placing a deep lusty kiss upon him much to his surprise. Her forked tongue danced across his and for some reason, he felt quite aroused by her. He did not miss a beat and returned the amorous embrace. The squad about them erupted in shouts of laughter and rude jests. Cobra broke away first and lightly pushed him away "You still owe me human and I fully intend to collect that debt." More jests and outbursts from the warriors directed at Bargavon.

As all settled back into pre-run procedures, Smiling Gold explained to Bargavon that his body was quite wounded and the fact he was already missing a fragment that Bargavon referred to the Dark Warrior. The medics did not have enough of his essence to work with and they thought they were going to lose him. Smiling Gold politely declined what would happen in the event that they did lose him except that it is quite a setback for a soul. Cobra had volunteered to offer up some of her own essence to fill in what was missing in Bargavon's structure. It was like an Essence transplant or transfusion. Cobra's power and essence would be diminished from what she was but in a way it elevated her Karma. A hell spawned devil sacrificing her own substance to help a human was probably a first of its kind. Further conversation was interrupted by Big Blue barging between them.

"Listen Medregorian, welcome back, but if you ever purposely pull a fuck up like you did on your last run with us, I will make sure we leave you to whatever fate could befall you in one of the dark realms. Am I clear warrior?" said Big Blue leaning his massive rhino like frame over Bargavon, his words literally snorted out of angry flared nostrils.

"I am quite clear, Sir. I will not fail the company again," replied Bargavon, his words were sincere. The Commander strode by at that moment, his golden armored mass made Big Blue look short. He stopped and leveled his gaze at Bargavon for a moment, his deep impenetrable eyes bored through Bargavon and seemed to peer into every crack, crevasse and recess of his mind and soul. Big Blue turned and said something quietly to the Commander, who never lifted his gaze from Bargavon. When he finished, the Commander turned and continued down the walkway between the warrior filled benches that paralleled it to either side. Big Blue turned back and started working through the deployment plan for the upcoming run, setting retrieval teams and fire squads. Bargavon would be teamed with Cobra on a retrieval team. He found it odd they were the only two. Everyone else was assigned to a fire squad.

Cobra came over to sit by him. She still radiated a faint aura of sexuality, but it was time to prepare for battle and Bargavon always marveled at how her features that could seem to exude such feminine sexuality could transform into a sharp fierceness, her scales fine as they were, thicken and harden, her hands became more claw like, the talons thicker, stronger. Her body seemed to sharpen the curves into panther like muscularity, her jaw thickened and at times one could see a fine ripple of flame trace her spine from her head to her tail.

"So, going to Hell today? Ever miss it, Cobra?" said Bargavon trying to start a conversation to break his own awkwardness with her.

Cobra turned slowly toward him, her fanged smile broke out from her grim look. "I spent over a thousand of your human years trying to get out of it. I never like Hell runs. It always makes me feel I'll get trapped back there again. Imagine hating where you were born or in my case created, spending millennia doing the same task over and over for an overlord who treats you no better than the lowliest spawn. Knowing that is all you will ever be until Hell comes to an end if ever. I was a slave created for one purpose."

"What was it?" inquired Bargavon.

"Retrievals." She replied with an evil laugh. "My overlord sent me into the Dense to seduce wicked men in their dreams and pull their souls either then or at death down into Hell where my master fed upon their torment."

Bargavon looked her up and down for even when she was not preparing for battle, no human would mistake her for other than a monster. Sensing his disbelief Cobra continued, "I didn't go like this. I chose guises that were so enticing they never said no." Changing the subject, Cobra looked about and seeing that the Commander and Big Blue were not nearby and the others of the squad were concentrating on their own preparations, she leaned into Bargavon and whispered low, "I overheard the Commander and Big Blue. There is only one retrieval on this run. It must be a high value one. Everybody else in all the squads are on fire teams except you and me."

"Has this ever happened before?"

"Not in a long time," Cobra said absently, her thoughts drifting back. The ship dropped and hit a swell, then another, then a series of long drops. Bargavon never could get use to the deep drops, his white knuckles betrayed his tenseness. Across from him, Big Red had fallen asleep, bearded chin on chest, his massive chorded forearms folded across his mailed torso. Next to him, Gage was trying to light his cigar, the match kept missing due to the buck and roll of the ship. Chant sat on Bargavon's left, his deep humming had a soothing and calming quality to it. Brass and Bronze were still trying to buckle each other's armor up. Ash and Corona sat quietly, unperturbed and motionless.

The Dark Warrior sat outside the barrier. A barrier he could not penetrate and no door or gate was open to him. He was not recognized as some lost soul to torment. He was but a fragment, a shard that sought closure for even he, the Dark Warrior had lost his sense of vengeful hate. He knew that part of him named Bargavon still rode with the company for he had seen him from afar. Eventually, he would have to face this.

Long had he journeyed across vast tracts of the Universe looking for this place. There were many like it in multitudes of forms throughout the vast expanses, prisons of torment, pain, anguish, loneliness, despair and darkness. But it was this one that held a soul he sought. He wanted to be there when it happened for he knew this happening would take place whether it be a thousand years, a thousand lifetimes or a thousand ages. What was time to the Dark Warrior? He had eternity, and so did everybody else.

In the gloomy depth a piercing column of light, like a concentrated beam of sunlight powered down through the gloom and broke open a hole in the barrier. Those that rode this column of light had authorization to do so. The local denizens were none too happy about this. The Dark Warrior made his way across the surface of the barrier toward the gap and the column of light. As he reached it he had to shield his face for the light's vibration seem to burn his very essence. So painful was the light he backed away to consider another plan of action. As he pondered various schemes of action, he saw something emerge from the gap. It growled and then barked sharply several times. His schemes dissipated then and there, he knew what he had to do. Feeling piercing white-hot pain shriek through every fiber of his being, the Dark Warrior plunged into the gap, directly into the column of light and down into one of the realms of Hell.

The Company was filing through one of the endless volcanic crevasses of one of the planes of Hell. The rock was volcanic, and the ground simply crushed blackened cinder. They wound their way down and down deep towards some vast yawning pit of blackness and despair. Screams and roars echoed forth but the company advanced forward undeterred. It was just another run in the vastness of the dark terrible cul-de-sacs in the vastness of the Universe.

The descent ended in a pit with high walls that went seemingly up forever. It was very dark and the air hung heavy and thick with pain and horror. It seemed as if a light sprinkle of rain fell about the place like a humid cave, but the liquid was of blood. It began to coat the armor of the company adding to their already grim aura. In the thickness of the gloom cries of terror and despair mixed with the throaty sighs and grunts of satisfaction of the devils feeding upon the terror, pain and despair of the damned sentenced here.

They spread out into the gloomy blood mist that saturated the air. Big Blue had teamed Bargavon with Cobra for the retrieval which was odd since Cobra's signature and essence made for the wrong mix. She was a devil and not even the lost and damned souls would confuse her for what she was. Bargavon's contemplation on the subject soon had an answer.

The Commander stopped and turned toward Bargavon. His golden armor coated dark red from the blood rain. His voice as always contained the power of earthquakes and tidal waves filtered down to a manageable roar that Bargavon's human mind deciphered as language (barely). "This retrieval is very important for you. It is necessary you retrieve your mark no matter what. The devil lord we face today is extremely dangerous and it may take all we have. I have faced him once before and his power is great. Do your job. Trust your heart, but do not trust your perceptions. They will deceive and betray you."

Bargavon simply nodded. After retrieving a score of people, he was quite proficient in the procedure. Some were even people he had known and he was able to extract them and get them to the Aperture without incident, he was not sure why this run could be different or why the Commander spoke to him personally, but he soon found out why.

The squad crunched along through the blood covered cinders. The sounds of intermittent combat sounded occasionally the gloom, devils were present. *Probably just the minor wretches and lower devil spawn,* thought Bargavon. The thick blood mist gave way to an open pocket of ground in the vast pit. Here the red mist drifted across the ground in sickly wisps. A short distance away sat a devil of great size, easily twice the size of the Commander. A mountain of muscle, thick bristly black hair sprouted from a powerfully thick torso. The head of was mix of a great ape and a ram. His eyes, however, were that of a fly. The visage was horrifying. His long muscular arms ended in powerful claws. The beast sat on what appeared to be a throne of skulls and bones, impossibly melted and fused into one another. What made it more horrifying was that the skulls emitted groans and cries of pain as if still imbued with life. Before him stood a score of powerful and dangerous looking minions, his servants and soldiers. They themselves were armed with weapons of jagged black metal of unusual shapes. They took various forms, but all were clad in black metal and strips of petrified bone.

"Belxerus, the Abominable Lord of the Blood Mist Wastes." Growled Big Blue, his massive fists flexed and squeezed hard upon the shaft of his weapon. Its leather like wrapping creaked. Big Red could be heard sucking in a deep breath, his breathing dropping into a pre- berserk state. Bargavon could see other squads and teams slowly stepping out from the gloom forming a battle line, at the front the towering visage of the Commander.

A familiar pull, an almost magnetic feeling pulled at Bargavon. The sensation that his retrieval mark was near came upon him. It pulled his vison away from the devil lord and his minions to a couple of forms off to the side. The scene was so traumatic it took Bargavon a few seconds to recover. At the same time he felt the devil lord Belxerus voice violate his mind. His words felt like filth, decay and agony pouring like sickly ichor through his conscious, "Do you like what I made for your Bargavon of Medregor. When I overcome your comrades today, I will make you watch this for eternity and feast upon your torment."

There before him, Prince Zhahir was raping Krin. He was looking at Bargavon and laughing. Krin looked at him, her face contorted in pain, humiliation and defeat. Tears poured down her face. "Save me please," she sobbed

Zhahir pulled her hair and cuffed her head from behind. He continued his animalistic pace into her all the while his eyes were locked on Bargavon. The prince exuded an aura of hate, lust and a delight in Bargavon's shock and horror.

Bargavon vaguely heard Big Blue next to him. "You got this, right?"

"Yeah. Got it, Sir." Bargavon heard himself say as if it came from a distance outside him. He felt held in place as the world around him erupted in a thunderous rupture of combat. The devils and the company ran across the blackened ground and collided in a cacophony of crunching metal, bone, clashing weapons, roars and yells, deep thudding impacts, the crackle of flame, flashing light, and the splattering of blood and ichor. In his mind the laughter of a devil lord, in complete delight at the horror Bargavon faced. He could feel himself slowly being drained, as if the Belxerus was feeding off Bargavon's horror and gaining power from it.

Prince Zhivar laughed at Bargavon's indecision, "I took your friend's life Bargavon, remember? Poor little Dev, so sweet he was. I so enjoyed the feeling of his life draining away, his blood pouring over my hands when I slit his throat on the training grounds. First Kill right? I bet you just died a little inside watching me do that to him. Just like when I had your sweet wife and your father murdered. You couldn't do anything then either. And now, here in the bowels of Hell itself I am still taking from you. Your slut is serving my desires very well. I can see why you liked this whore, but she's all mine now." Zhahir laughed again never halting his lust filled rhythm.

Bargavon was trying to work out the situation in his mind that made sense of what he was seeing. *Krin was a strong woman, a whelp like Zhahir could never dominate her like that, she was too strong, this is not like her. Why would she be here anyway, that makes.....*"

A diabolical voice in his head was so bombastic it drowned out his own thought, "Makes all the sense in the world for you caused all this ruin. You did this Bargavon."

Bargavon was so transfixed by what was before him that a devil came from the side and nearly took off Bargavon's head with a multi-bladed polearm, but his blow was diverted by Valor the dog who came from nowhere and threw his body in front of the blade and took the blow. The dog fell upon the cinders in a ragged dying heap. Bargavon drew forth his blade at last and reached for his ax to face off with this devil. The combat between them was intense. These minions were powerful and Bargavon was hard pressed with this one, but he drove forward as the devil reared back and with both arms overhead to bring down a death blow upon him. His midsection exposed, Bargavon dew both sword and ax blade across it opening him up under its carapace of bone armor. Black ichor poured forth freely and it stumbled back. Bargavon's ax thudded deep into its chest with such unbridled fury and force it puncturing through the metal plate like tin can. The devil dropped.

Several of the lesser spawn had entered the fray, being drawn into the pit by the magnetic pull of violence and horror. Gage's weapon lit the area up with a dozen violent flashes of crackling bright light and these dark figures exploded in fragments and arcing globs of ichor. Behind Bargavon, Big Red's ax swept through a smaller spawn cutting him completely in half before burying deep into the flank of a massive devil, twice his size. Big Blue had one pinned upon the ground, his massive blue claws pulling it apart while a second smaller devil spawn had hopped upon Blues pack and was trying to wedge a twisted black spike between his armor plates. Brass, Bronze and Chant were already back to back surrounded by twice their number in a maelstrom of violence. Ash's body was of self-immolated spectral fire and arcs of lightning, his body in a death grapple with another of the larger bodyguards, the spectral fire lancing up the body of his opponent.

Cobra stood nearby and clutched a leaping spawn out of the air within her grasp and slammed it into the blood soaked ground. "You want to hurry up human. This isn't going to get easier." She hissed

Bargavon was literally weak, the sick hopelessness, the horror of what lay before him mixed with the taunting of the devil lord in his mind was breaking down even his iron will. He staggered over to Zhahir. He had to retrieve him no matter what. *This has to end even though I hate him more than anything. Why isn't he willing to go? He has been here for a long time if I was called in to retrieve him. This is not making sense.*

"You can't do it Bargavon. Your hate is too strong and this is how you'll remain for eternity. This is how you will suffer for all you have done," said Prince Zhahir triumphantly. He tossed Krin's naked form aside and stalked around Bargavon, his form passed through Cobra like a ghost who was standing by. Being Bargavon's mark meant none other in the Company could assist until Bargavon made the initial rescue.

"Come on, grab that piece of shit and let's go!" said Cobra angrily, returning her attention back to stabbing the life out of the spawn she slammed to the ground. Two more leaped at her and her panther like movements avoided their claws while simultaneously lancing one through the mouth with a wide bladed polearm she had picked off a dead bodyguard.

Bargavon had fallen to his knees, he looked to the dog Valor, who had given his life to save his, to Krin, the only woman he had given his heart to, laying upon the bloody cinders, her eyes pleaded for Bargavon to save her. The naked and blood covered prince stalked over to her and roughly grabbed her up by the throat and dragged her to just out of reach of Bargavon.

"You cannot harm me here. I belong here, fucking your slut for eternity and enjoying every minute of the anguish you will bear," smiled the prince, jubilant. He stopped choking Krin long enough to stretch his arms out in victory. "All the pain, suffering and death you caused in your meaningless life in the Dense serving me, serving the Empire. How many woman have you taken? Just part of the spoils of war, eh Captain? How many innocents died by your own hand? Think of all those men, woman and children in the name of my Empire. You belong here to suffer, and so you shall! Look about, look about to your doom, your eternity!"

"Any fucking time you want to get to that retrieval would be appreciated," yelled Big Red staggering back from the onslaught of the massive devil. Gage fought just past him, down on one knee with three devil spawn hammering at him, his heavy jagged blade stabbing upward at close range spilling out the guts of one of his attackers. The Company was starting to collapse under the sheer weight and ferocity of their attackers. The Commander was in personal combat with Belxerus, the two massive foes swinging into each other with unbridled violence. Around them Company warriors and devil guards were in a churning melee.

Prince Zhahir went back to Krin and laid her limp form upon a rock. "I think I'll have her this way now." He looked down and gave a dramatic gesture of concern, "My dear, you look uncomfortable, here let me get you a pillow." From behind the rock he drew forth a decapitated head. "How is this for a pillow Bargavon?" laughed Prince Zhaihir. It was the decapitated head of Dev.

Bargavon lurched forward, his soul a cacophony of immense hate, loss, despair, hopelessness and sick horror. *I will retrieve you. I will retrieve you.* Like a mantra Baragvon flooded his mind against the tsunami of dark thoughts and emotions. Again, he stumbled and fell, his body fighting the repulsion of horror that lay before him. *Stay down and let me feed, You are mine!* Poured Belxerus's poison words in his mind

"Fuck, the Commander has fallen! Squad to me, to the Commander!" bellowed Big Blue staggering toward the epicenter of combat. The rhino like warrior's armor was rent in places and Bargavon could see horrible wounds upon his squad leader. His comrades were no better. All of them looked wounded but still they fought on. Big Red had gone berserk, his Northman rage sent him into a fury of arcing death with his ax, seemingly unaffected by the half dozen blackened barbed shafts piercing his torso. Smiling Gold was working on the downed form of Ash. Corona stood by fending off the unrelenting attacks of waves of spawn and devil soldiers. So many his halo cast was dimmed by their sheer numbers. Beyond him the crumpled golden form of the Commander was being hammered down by the devil lord. Nearby, Cobra skewered a devil with the polearm one had dropped earlier. Only she stayed to protect Bargavon who was stumbling and half crawling to the horror before him.

"We're out of time human. I don't want to take residence here again," yelled Cobra, this time her voice carried great concern.

Bargavon made one last lunge at Prince Zhahir, who was placing the decapitated head under Krin's neck. His hands slipped right through him as if he were a ghost.

"What? But how?" gasped Bargavon incredulously. His eyes widened in disbelief.

Prince Zhahir looked down at Bargavon. "Oh, I see you wanted a closer look. You are such a depraved lost soul. You belong here."

"I don't understand. You're my mark. I'm supposed to retrieve you," stammered Bargavon, all hope ebbing out of him. He dropped to both knees defeated at last. *None of this makes sense, Krin, Dev, they shouldn't be here.* A confused daze washed over him, the voice of Belxerus continued unabated in his mind.

"Wrong. You were meant to be here for eternity to witness this, even as I placed your physical form in the prison back in the Dense. It all worked out so perfectly." Prince Zhahir laughed and began to lower himself on Krin.

I deserve all of this, and I am truly sorry for all of it. The thought was one of quiet finality within the mind of Bargavon. It was over.

A low growl could be heard of from behind him, Bargavon turned to see Valor coming his way, his front paws clawing their way across the cinders, his back end ruined, his guts pulling behind him but despite this there was a strange happiness and love for his master in his eyes as they locked upon Bargavon. His tail wagged as best it could. Faithful until the end, it would share the doom with his master. It looked to Bargavon and then behind it, wagging its tail.

From the gloom of bloody mist emerged a silhouette of sheer blackness. Its eyes glowed a blazing red, no definitive features were there upon it, but it was the form of Bargavon.

It strode through the battlefield directly toward Zhahir, the devils and spawn at first ignored it thinking it was one of their own. Cobra was being beaten down by two of Belxerus's bodyguards. The Dark Warrior's weapons came out as he approached. A night black ax appeared in his right hand, a longsword of the same impenetrable blackness in the other. A low menacing growl like boulders tumbling down a mountain rose into a primal roar of a battle, his sharp tooth mouth opened in the black form, his eyes blazing fiery red death.

The two devil bodyguards realized too late that the Dark Warrior was not one of them. The first large beast from hell crumpled under a hail of ax and sword blows that sent liquid towers of ichor streaming upward to meet the blood red mist. The second bodyguard flung Cobra down and lunged at this new foe. Their weapons met and struck sparks, their bodies slammed into each other. Despite the devil's larger mass, its efforts to drive back his foe were stopped dead. The Dark Warrior embodied much of the dark malice and hate of Bargavon and this power appeared nearly unstoppable. The fight was brief and terrible to behold and ended suddenly as the devil's head was nearly decapitated and hung oddly by a few strands of sinew as the rest of its bulk dropped and flopped about reflexively.

Cobra had crawled her way next to Bargavon and the dog. She had been badly wounded and was coughing up black blood. She smiled at Bargavon and looked back at the Dark Warrior as he was ending the second bodyguard's ability to be anything other than an unanimated husk.

"Is that your so called broken fragment they have been talking about? He's terribly beautiful. Perhaps you could introduce me to him." Her snake like eyes closed and for once her face appeared peaceful. She collapsed against the bloody cinders and no longer moved.

The Dark Warrior strode up to Bargavon and looked down. "Valor found me. Let's end this together," he said as a hollow rasp of grating stone upon metal.

The form of Zhahir for the first time lost its sense of confidence. It moved away from Krin, it wavered and shrunk back. From across the battlefield a terrible roar resounded. It came from Belxerus, who looked up from the crumpled form of the Commander he had been pummeling with his great claws. Around him his minions seemed to be momentarily confused.

Bargavon jumped to his feet quickly, the hope suddenly broke through the aura of despair about him. Belxerus' mental hold was broken in his mind. He looked to Prince Zhahir, who was slowly starting to back up from Krin upon the rock and then back at the Dark Warrior who was moving up beside him.

"It's a fucking trick! An illusion! The Devil lord is feeding on my pain and fear from a fucking illusion!" sneered Bargavon, his anger surging through his veins. "We both have to retrieve this son of a bitch."

"I know," hissed the Dark Warrior, sheathing his weapons and starting towards Zhahir. He never made it. Like a sudden tidal wave of muscular blackness the great form of Belxerus smashed into the Dark Warrior sending him tumbling like a rag doll through the field of broken bodies.

"No! This is my domain!" roared Belxerus drowning out the rest of the sounds of battle about them.

Bargavon reached for his sword and ax. He stood boldly before the behemoth before him. "I have been the pawn of an Empire and it has been my ruin. I will not be the amusement

227

for a Devil!" said Bargavon his words charged with molten malice and anger.

The Devil-lord laughed "You alone cannot stop me puny human."

"I am no longer alone," replied Bargavon, his voice seethed with dark menace, pointing behind Belxerus with his sword.

Belxerus turned to see the Dark Warrior leaping out of the blood mist, his sword and ax raised above him, his eyes burned a violent red and his maw a shape of jagged white sharpness. His weapons sunk deep into the massive hide. Belxerus roared and Bargavon plowed into his flanks driving a hail of his own sword and ax blows into a wall of scale and bristling fur.

The storm of hate, brutal violence, and raw power between the devil-lord and his two sword and ax armed assailants became the center point for which the rest of the battle swirled around. Claws rent mail and ripped into flesh, spilling red blood of both versions of Bargavon. Sword and ax hacked gapping wounds from which flowed out the blackest of foul ichor. Belxerus smashed and slammed down the Dark Warrior and Bargavon with such powerful force the ground sent up a spray of blood and ichor coated cinders and blackened crust. Still they rose, both feeding off each other, their rage, their hate, the unbridled power here in a realm where those qualities were maximized. Split of body, they were now one of thought, their focus narrowed to destruction to the foe before them. Together now, they would never stop.

A massive backhand sent Bargavon reeling back again, blood was flowing from deep gashes in so many places he did not know where one wound started and another ended. Anger anesthetized his pain. He felt nothing. He started back toward Belxerus, who now hobbled about as one great cloven foot dangled only by a few thick tendons. He was trying to pivot to grab at the Dark Warrior, who was working to chop through the remainder with his blades.

A great clawed hand grabbed him from behind. Bargavon whirled about, but saw it was Big Blue. His face was half ruined. The faceplates on one side were cleaved and the tissue was torn away gruesomely exposing his bleeding gums, and his lower teeth.

"Your job is to retrieve, Warrior! Retrieve dammit!" the rhino like creature roared, his speech garbled by the horrible facial wound.

"Belxerus!" bellowed Bargavon back, his rage had unhinged him.

"Look!" Big Blue roared back, pointing to Zhahir who was skulking way toward the shadows at the edge of the pit. "Now go!"

Bargavon ran to Belxerus and knocked the Dark Warrior out of the way from being stomped by the uninjured cloven hoof. As they rolled out of the way they turned to see Big Blue impale Belxerus through the stomach with his polearm, at the same time the Commander had leaped up on the devil lords back and grappled at his maw, trying to force it open and crack the great jaws. Others of the company closed in driving weapon or fired rounds into the great beast at expense of their own personal protection for the devil guards and minions were still great in number.

Bargavon pointed to Zhahir. "Belxerus is sending him away, so we can't retrieve him." The Dark Warrior understood and they both sprinted across the blood-soaked ground. They overtook the Prince who tried to shrink back from their grasp. Bargavon felt the body of his retrieval at last for they were both needed to complete the capture. The Prince tried to wrestle away but it was useless against Bargavon's vice like grip as well as the grip of the dark aspect of himself. They drug him across the field of battle toward the path upward to the ship.

Bargavon looked back one last time to where Krin's battered body lay. It was as he expected. Nothing was there. The illusion had been broken. Smiling Gold was bending down to check the prone unmoving form of Cobra and the dog Valor. Brass and Bronze stood near him lighting up the area with their weapons, devil spawn exploded in sparks and black chunks.

Belxerus had thrown off the Commander who was on his back, a stalagmite of twisted rock was impaled through him, still he fought, his gauntleted fists breaking the iron hard bones of Belxerus's taloned fingers that tried to reach through his faceguards. There were bodies of fellow warriors prone and unmoving strewn across the field. Big Blue stood upon the dead carcass of a great devil valiantly rallying the rest of the warriors that stood in what looked like a final stand.

A few of the warriors from another squad that were left in a rear guard flanked Bargavon and the Dark Warrior providing protection on the way up the steep path.

"How did you know about the retrieval?" inquired Bargavon, his voice came out as a gasping exhalations, his injuries started to emerge upon his awareness

"Dev told me." The Dark Warrior said simply.

"You found Dev?"

"You are not the only one wandering about in the dark wanting answers, wanting relief, closure, peace," breathed the

Dark Warrior heavily, his gravelly voice was tinged with fatigue.

Majestic Carnage was with this squad. He was second in command to the Commander. Almost as massive and quite tall, this individual was covered in blue and plate heavy plate. His helm was of the same strange heavy metal and the front was just a vertical slit for vision. What he had for eyes behind it Bargavon had never seen for his helm was always on. He had four powerful metal clad arms that hung like articulated battering rams. "Keep moving with the retrieval, I apparently need to retrieve the Company," boomed his voice with a deep confident resonance.

Bargavon did not see what took place moments later but heard several explosions and the rocks around him lit up with flashes of blue-white light and the blood mist seemed to glow with phosphorescence for several seconds.

"Cobra, Valor, the Commander, so many of the Company went down," said Bargavon suddenly as the reality of the battle just hit him full force. He stopped on the path and looked back into the bloody mist filled pit. The last of the blue-white phosphorescence faded. Emerging from the bloody gloom strode Smiling Gold with Cobra draped over his shoulder. In his other arm, he carried Valor who still panted breaths and licked his tongue up at Smiling Gold's faceplate. Behind him lumbered Big Blue supporting the Commander under one arm, Majestic Carnage, was under the other. Company warriors were coming up from behind them, many wounded or carrying comrades.

"Bargavon Human, quit standing there dawdling! You have one job to do on this drop. Get that retrieval to the ship! That goes for you too black phantom fragment," bellowed Big

Blue, half his head and neck armor were torn away revealing deep claw wounds and blood streaming out in torrents as he spoke.

The Commander's wounds looked grave. He was a wrecked hulk. Blood the color of deep metallic blue poured forth from several deep wounds and a trail of it followed him. His golden armor was mangled and torn or in places sheared away revealing an outwardly massive muscular body that seemed to draw one's vision into it revealing a deep spatial midnight blue sea reflecting slow spirals of stars upon the surface. A great stain of his shimmering blood marked his path.

The rearguard of the Company was led by Big Red, the Northman berserker whose rage fueled ax swings cleared the devil minions and the spawn away in great swaths. What few weapons or claws pierced his mail or cleaved across his forearms were like scratches to him. He felt nothing, only berserk rage. The reserve squad arrived. Fresh warriors smashed against the black horde that tried to make their way up out of the pit. The Baboonish warrior Chant lumbered within the rear guard. His chanting seemed to make the tattoos upon his bulky frame throb and glow silver. The pace of throbbing increased as his chanting got louder until his maw opened to emit a sonic roar that sheared the bodies of a score of the devil horde before him into atomized black dust. After that there was little pursuit and the Company made their way to the ship.

From deep within the blood mist of the black pit, the devil lord Belxerus beat upon the blackened crust of the pit floor in frustration and anger. He bellowed and screamed, yelled forth curses and unholy words that would instantly kill more fragile lifeforms than the warriors of the Company. He had lost not just Zhahir but also the soul of Bargavon who's torment would have fed Belxerus's appetite for a long time.

The exhausted and wounded warriors fell onto their benches or onto the floor of the ship. Smiling Gold along with the healers and medics within the ship got to work on them, triaging the warriors and aiding those the most wounded. It was a chaotic flurry of activity. The ramp was drawn up and there was a feeling of lift in the hull.

Prince Zhahir sat between Bargavon and his black twin. Both said nothing. They were spent physically, emotionally and spiritually. Zhahir sat in stunned silence. To him, he had endured a centuries upon centuries of hellish torment and Belxerus was no longer controlling him. Big Red had returned to a calm state, his bloodlust had been satisfied. It was only now he realized he had jagged bolts piercing his mail that was covered equally in his own blood and the black ichor of his kills. Ichor covered nearly every inch of him and his great ax. He smiled across as Bargavon, revealing that the ichor splatter had worked its way into his mouth as well.

"So there you both are, huh?" said Big Red grinning and pointing to Bargavon and the Dark Warrior. "What do you make of this Gage?"

Gage stood next to Big Red and reached up to hold onto an overhead support strut. "Red, I'm just a grunt. I don't understand half this shit out here." He looked over at the bench at Bargavon. "Maybe Smiling Gold can kind of smoosh them both back together or something."

Big Blue lumbered in at that moment after being worked on by the medics. Half his face and head were wrapped up from the wounds he suffered. "Commander's going to make it I think, I can't believe how much he took from Belxerus.

That was the hairiest drop we ever had." He stopped talking and then got quiet, his one rhino like eye rested on Bargavon for several moments. The commotion of warriors cleaning and storing equipment and weapons, the cries of the wounded being worked on by the medics and the hum and thump of the hull as it passed through regions to their destination to drop off their retrieval all seemed to dim to a muffled quiet.

To Bargavon all this seemed to have a dream-like quality. Big Blue looked down at him, his face serious and thoughtful. The rest of the squad was gathering around; Brass, Bronze, Chant, Ash, Corona, Cobra being supported by Smiling Gold. Big Red remained seated, a medic was removing the bolts and he was trying not to wince. Behind them loomed the massive form of the Commander who took a seat. He was weak and very wounded. The medics were scolding him for getting up out of the medical bay and continued to patch up his wounds with temporary compresses. He said nothing but held out a massive hand that looked black as space filled with nebula and clusters of swirling stars. Bargavon clasped it with his own, so small within the Commanders grasp. His eyes looked into Bargavon who felt as if he were drawn up into their depths. He felt the communion of thought and emotion, meaning and understanding with that one moment. He felt the respect of the Commander, the shared hardships that they both have endured and will yet face, the bloody road that led them both to this moment and the redemption that they feel with each passing retrieval, each run into the dark places of the Universe where no one else dared to tread.

The ramp was opening up. They were not at the Aperture. Instead they were near a world, clouds drifted across great landmasses and great blue oceans. Bargavon sat there confused. They had always dropped off retrievals at the Aperture. He looked to the Commander and then to Big Blue.

"It's your world Bargavon. Down there your physical body still exists. You need to go back and complete your physical life," said Big Blue.

"But what of the retrieval? Zhahir, what of him?" said Bargavon, looking to Big Blue and then the Commander.

"He goes back to your world too. That was the orders given to me for this retrieval. He returns to a new life, one born in poverty and despair. Perhaps he experiences loss, heartache, pain, suffering, perhaps joy, love and happiness, perhaps every one of those. He is not ready for the Aperture. Maybe he is lifetimes away. It is not up to the Company to judge or for us to know. We just follow orders and work the drops and the runs." said the Commander, his voice resonant and powerful.

"Go on Warrior Bargavon, both of yourselves. Lead this retrieval out," said Big Blue stiffly. He then smiled and nodded.

Bargavon and the Dark Warrior walked toward the ramp holding the subdued Zhahir between them. As they passed through the crowd of warriors of Big Blue's squad, there was cheering and clapping, words of encouragement and of good luck. He saw the proud smiles of his comrades and as the world seemed to spread out before him and blur into mist he heard Big Red's voice boom out in the distance, "Don't think you're discharged from the Company Medregorian. We got a whole lot of runs to do yet together brother!"

There was a sense of movement, blurring mist, falling. Sun, clouds and light seemed to spin about causing him vertigo. He no longer felt Zhahir who seemed to vanish, instead the Dark Warrior was clasped arm and arm with him as they fell like stones.

I guess this is it then. Together.

Together then, came the reply, just a thought. Whether it was Bargavon or the Dark Warrior was irrelevant. They were now one in the same.

Chapter 13

Escape

Light poured across his face. Bargavon awoke on the floor of a filthy dark cell. Torchlight washed over him. Outside the iron bars of his cell was Vasardev working keys into the lock. Behind him in the torchlight were the faces of several loyal men from his units he was told were dead. Malibar his old lieutenant was leading them. *Strange*, thought Bargavon, *now it is I who am rescued, retrieved by my own men. It seems things have come full circle.*

The escape from the dungeons was a quick operation for it was further expedited by guards who were previous veterans of the army. They knew the allegations against Bargavon were false, especially coming from someone like Prince Zhahir who was quietly despised by many. The group made their way out of the prison joined by some of the guards that knew their life was forfeit when the prince finds out about the escape. They worked their way down to waiting boats at the base of the cliffs. Out in the bay under the blanket of night anchored the *Ghost Eagle*. She carried with her a full crew of men, men who were recently loyal Imperial marines and sailors, men who served under Captain Bargavon, now renegades for they escaped the trap Prince Zhahir set for them out at sea. A heroic tale that was retold to Bargavon over goblets of wine and tankards of ale at a future time when the *Ghost Eagle* sailed upon friendly waters.

Bargavon looked out from the deck of the war galley. Kathvitora was dotted with torches and lanterns that outlined it against the dark mountains that surrounded it and the great crescent bay before it. The dark moonless night would soon be ending and the cover it provided the crew would be lost. Men pulled hard at oars driving the craft out into the Arysissar Sea, getting as much distance between them and the imminent pursuit of Imperial Naval vessels.

The *Ghost Eagle* unfurled its sails and powered by oars sped off into the grayness of the coming dawn. Bargavon and these men were now outlaws of the Medregorian Empire. It was a big world and there were many places outside the Empire to find freedom, glory, gold and adventure. Untethered to the empire that trained and controlled them, their destinies now were in their own hands with Bargavon their chosen leader.

Epilogue

Bargavon propped his head up on his bedroll and looked up at the stars above. The gentle waves of the Arysissar Sea lapped against the wooden hull of The *Ghost Eagle* anchored in the protective cove at a port town along the Azillon Coast. He had returned to the ship after drinking more than his fair share of wine at the tavern. News had reached this far flung port at the edge of the Medregorian Empire that Prince Zhahir had died recently just after leaving Kathvitora on his way back to Wuxano where he was to rule his new principality. Some say he was poisoned by his younger brother Prince Vitore, who then replaced Zhahir, others say it was a Wuxani assassin. Yet another story mentioned he died of an opium overdose. It mattered not to Bargavon, he knew now Zhahir's death was just part of a bigger life cycle hidden from the normal perceptions of man.

The slow rocking of the ship, the gentle sea breeze and the wine were dragging Bargavon into sleep. Even the sound of the other men sleeping and the hushed tones of the men talking idly on watch did not keep Bargavon from slipping into his wine soaked slumber. He quite filly expected the type of sleep he had gotten use to again since his run into Hell to retrieve Zhahir almost two months ago. His were normal dreams or a night of blissful nothingness. No Veils to pass, runs with the Company, Jaguar Gods or other spiritual personages or landscapes to walk.

He awoke from a dream and found himself passing through the Veil. It had been a few months since he passed this way. There appearing before him in the darkness was a smudge of light that soon took the form of Valor. He was strong and healthy, his eyes bright and his tail wagged excitedly as he greeted Bargavon. He barked and indicated to Bargavon to follow him. They soon came to the dock. There was the ramp leading upward to the side of the familiar ship. Gage stood upon the ramp expecting him.

"Welcome back. I told Valor to get you. Big Blue and the squad will be happy to have you back."

"I thought I wasn't coming back until I died?" said Bargavon making his way up the ramp

"Died? Medregorian, how many times do you need reminding? You are not getting off that easy. Besides you were requested for this run," said Gage flicking cigar ash off into the darkness.

They entered into the hold. A round of greetings met him as he made his way over to his spot along the bench. The warriors were busy prepping arms and armor or stowing away gear, rummaging through packs or assisting others to busk on their gear.

"How's the Dense, Medregorian?" smiled Big Red slapping a heavy hand onto Bargavon's mailed shoulder

"You know, long periods of boredom broken up with harrowing moments of fighting, occasional warm embraces of women and more often the solace of wine and the pursuit of enough gold in our pouches. My men and I are wanted by the Empire. We're just making our way across the sea offering service as sell swords. You'd like it," responded Bargavon checking his sword and ax in their harnesses, "Where we going?"

"Ask them," said Big Red thumbing toward a cluster of figures to the center of the hold.

Bargavon stood up and peered past the crowd of warriors. There, he saw the massive form of the Commander in his golden armor talking with someone he couldn't see. When some men finally parted out of the way he saw who the Commander was talking too. The Jaguar God was sitting there, his large black feline face trained upward on the Commander. As if sensing being watched, the cat's gaze turned to meet Bargavon's. Behind him he vaguely heard the tail end of Big Blue conversation with Majestic Carnage "...really? Huh, this will be interesting."

About the Author

Travis Summerville is a first time author who enjoys spending his off hours in in such physical activities as playing with his dog, working out and practicing Qigong and Tibetan Burning Palm Kung Fu. Quieter moments are spent reading, meditating and other esoteric interests. He lives with his wife and two daughters in Michigan where he plays the part of a Physical Therapist in real life.

www.ingramcontent.com/pod-product-compliance
Lightning Source LLC
Chambersburg PA
CBHW070603130626
46556CB00001B/263